FIND A GAP

SEATTLE CASACADES
BOOK 5.5

C.M. KANE

COPYRIGHT

～

Editing & book design by Maggie Kern @ Ms.K Edits

Cover art by Golden Czermak @ FuriousFotog

BOOK 5.5

SEATTLE
CASCADES

DEDICATION

For all those who wish they were young enough, and all those who know they are.

PROLOGUE

Heather...

"Heather." Tiffany's voice came out of the video on my computer screen.

I'd watched the entire video when I was first contacted by her attorney and went to his office, but I hadn't been able to bring myself to watch it again. We were sisters. Not biologically, but in every other sense of the word. Hell, our birthdays were just two weeks apart, so we were practically twins. We met when we were in kindergarten, and we have been the absolute best friends our entire lives.

When her parents died when we were twelve, my parents adopted her. She didn't have any family, and if we hadn't taken her in, she would've ended up in the foster care system. I'd cried to my parents about how it wouldn't be fair for her to be shipped off to who-knew-where when she could just stay with us. I miss the innocence of that little girl I used to be.

"If you're watching this," she continued, "well, I guess my biggest adventure is now beginning. You know, the one that you can never share with your friends and family after you cross over to whatever awaits on the other side. I'm sure it was something stupid that

1

happened to me, but I couldn't stop seeking that next thrill. You know me, so that shouldn't surprise you."

At some point, I'd accepted the fact that Tiff would never grow out of her thrill for adventure. Sure, we did some wild things, but not anything dangerous. Now, at almost forty-four, she was gone. I had received everything she had—not much in the way of actual possessions because she lived on the road and out of a backpack. But her vlog, which had quite the following, as well as her finances, were all given to me. When I heard how much money she had coming in, I was in shock.

"I know that you like safety," she continued. "Staying home, getting a respectable job, and maybe even looking to settle down. But let me tell you what you're missing."

I'd gone to college just up the road from my parents' house and gotten a degree in business, but really, I was just looking for something to get me a simple job. I didn't want anything fancy, nothing that would pay hundreds of thousands of dollars, just something I could do to keep a roof over my head. I lived with my parents until I was twenty-seven when they suggested that they might like to use my room for an office of sorts. Because I hadn't had any bills, I saved absolutely everything I made, except for my car, insurance, and other things that were a necessity. I'd paid my parents a modest amount for rent, but they just put it toward the extras that it was costing to have me living there. It wasn't much, and they didn't need it. I just did it to feel like I was contributing to the household.

"There's something to be said for getting a rush from something dangerous," she said, and I could see the truth in that statement, even if it was a rush that didn't interest me in the least. "I'm not talking about all the wild things like running with the bulls or the terrifying things like climbing El Cap in Yosemite. Biking through the hills in France was a thrill and definitely something you would enjoy."

She was right in that I would love to go biking through France, but I didn't have a passport. Hell, I'd never even traveled out of the state of Illinois before. Tiff had been around the world a dozen times in the last fifteen or so years since she started her adventures.

"I've invited you to come with me a ton," she said, continuing her final message to me. "But now I'm going to give you an ultimatum. I've made a decent amount of money doing this adventure vlog, which you now have access to. I set aside enough money so that, when this eventually happened, you would be able to take a full year to do some adventuring yourself. You don't need to do anything extreme, but you do have to get out of Harrisburg. There's a whole wide world out here, and you should experience it before it's too late."

The tears had started pretty early in my watching of the video, and now they were running down my face in rivers. She was right about me needing to get out of the town where I grew up, but I didn't want to do all the crazy things she had. I wasn't built like her. I was built to stay rooted to where I was born. Still, the thought of actually going somewhere and seeing something besides my little place was enticing.

"I've made a list of places in the US where you can go," she continued. "I've made friends all over the world, but these places are where I started my adventure. There are cities that you need to experience, and I think you'll enjoy the ones I've selected. One year is all I'm asking you for. You can give me that. While I doubt you'll do everything I did or go to all the places I have, I want you to take this gift and explore the world. I love you, ya dork, and hope you'll find everything you never knew you wanted out here on the road."

The video faded to black, and I stared at the screen. I'd received the news that she had died on Valentine's Day. It wasn't exactly the best day for me, anyway, but now it was marked with the thought of her death. She was the one who had boyfriends and girlfriends from all over the world. I'd had one in high school, but he'd turned out to be a jerk. I hooked up a bit in college, but nothing ever felt like it was worth spending time doing. It never seemed like a big deal to me, and that hadn't changed since I bought my house. Still, the fact that my soul sister died, and on that specific day, made it seem like it was an even worse day than before.

I had a file folder with a list of places, as well as all the access to the back side of her website. She'd set up an automatic post that her attorney had released after notifying me of her passing, letting her followers know that she had passed away and that her best friend was going to take over the reins. I'd followed her adventures online, but never in a million years thought she'd send me on a quest in her stead. Now, though, I had the funds, the list of places, and enough encouragement to do it.

Three weeks ago, my best friend was flying off to Argentina to go paragliding. She'd done it a number of times before, and she wanted to do it again. I can't fault anyone for her death. It wasn't a failure of equipment, human error, or something to do with her travels. No. She had an undiagnosed aneurysm that burst in her aortic tract just above her heart. She didn't see it coming. No one did. It feels like it would be selfish to not do what she wanted me to, so I'd put in a request for a sabbatical. One year. I could give up my comfortable, boring life for one year just to remember her.

I cleaned myself up, put on some makeup, and set up the phone her attorney had given me for this specific purpose on the kitchen table, in the little stand she'd used for her own videos. As much as I hated the idea of people seeing me, I knew that she would be proud of me if I actually took her challenge to heart. So, instead of running from it, I sat my happy ass down and did the hardest thing I'd ever done in my life. I took a video of myself to share on the internet.

"I know it's not what you're used to," I said into the phone. "But this is me, Heather, absolute best friend and sister to your beloved Tiffany. I'm going to go on an adventure, and I'm bringing you with me. I won't do nearly as much as she did, and my videos are probably going to be entirely too boring. But I promised her that one day I would adventure, and in her memory, I'm going to do just that. She was the bravest person I knew, and I hope that she's somewhere out there watching me take this risk, take her challenge to heart, and get out of my comfort zone. Here goes nothing."

CHAPTER ONE

Heather...

In two months, I had done the unthinkable. Well, unthinkable for me, anyway. I had left my comfortable home, my boring job, and the town where I was born and grew up. Now, I was on a plane and heading to Seattle. The rules my friend gave me were simple. See the world, find something exciting where ever I went, and have fun. No more than four weeks, no less than two, and each place had to be somewhere new.

When my parents drove me to Chicago, where I checked into the Hilton Garden Hotel downtown, they told me they were proud of me. They wanted to make sure I did this adventure, knowing that it was a struggle. We had dinner before they headed back home.

While the hotel wasn't very expensive, it was still more than what I would normally have paid for a hotel. That was the lie I told myself, anyway, because the truth was, I hadn't stayed in a hotel since I was in college, and Tiffany and I went up to the big city for an adventure. It wasn't the kind of adventures she ended up going on recently, but we did go see a play, went to some of the touristy places, and had a great time.

The first couple of days were hard, but I forced myself to go out

5

and see some things. I asked the concierge where to go, explaining I was on a mission from a friend to adventure in her memory. He gave me some ideas of where to see things that weren't as touristy but were still interesting. I had no idea there were so many things to see and do within a short drive from my house.

Now, though, I was holding the armrest of the first-class seat I'd booked for this flight and freaking out about the whole thing.

"Hey," the woman sitting next to me said. "First time flying?"

"Is it that obvious?" I asked.

"At least you're in first class," she said. "If you were in coach, you wouldn't get free booze."

I wanted to cry, wanted to scream, wanted to bolt off the airplane, and run back to my safe place. But I didn't. No, I'd promised Tiff and myself that I would do what she suggested and just try it for a year. Who knew? Maybe I'd end up loving it so much that I'd follow in her footsteps.

"What are you heading to Seattle for?" she asked as the door to the plane, my only escape route, was closed and locked.

"I'm going on an adventure," I said. "By orders of my best friend."

"Good for you," she said. "And good for your friend to encourage you to do it."

"I just wish she was with me," I said.

"She too busy?"

"She died," I said, and then realized how terrible that was. "She had an aneurysm and passed away a couple of months ago. Her whole life was an adventure, and her dying wish and challenge to me was to at least see part of this big world."

"I'm sorry she's gone," she said. "But I bet she'd be real proud of you for following in her footsteps."

"I think she would," I said.

Four and a half hours later, the pilot came over the intercom and said that we would be landing soon in Seattle. He said that the weather was mild with some overcast, but that sun was expected for the next couple of days. I'd had two drinks on the flight, which was more than I'd had in the last five years, but I felt much more relaxed as the plane tipped and we started the landing process.

My seatmate was kind, telling me about her granddaughter, who she was going to meet for the first time in person, and all about the travels that she'd done in her life. As much as my parents would have liked it, I never wanted to have kids. They were too messy, too loud, and too much responsibility for me to take on. I'd thought about it, but now, at my age, finding someone to have kids with, or even thinking about having kids, was well in my past.

"Take my card," my neighbor said, handing over the small rectangle with her contact information on it. "If you don't know what to do or want to have someone come with you, don't hesitate to call or text me. I love a good adventure and would be happy to show you around. But," she added when I went to thank her. "Do *not* feel obligated to contact me. I won't feel bad if I don't hear from you. I'll just assume you're out having the time of your life."

"Thanks," I said, then pulled out one of the cards Tiff's attorney gave me. "My friend created a vlog to share her adventures with the world. I'm now in charge of it, so you can check it out if you want and see what I decide to do. Please be kind, though, because my videos are so much simpler than hers were."

"I'm sure you're great," she said, and I believed her.

Just then, the plane landed, giving a little bounce before settling on the ground where the brakes were thrown, and we were all pushed forward by the inertia of the sudden deceleration.

"Ladies and gentlemen," the flight attendant said. "I'd like to be the first to welcome you to Seattle. Please remain seated until we have parked at the gate, and the pilot has turned off the seatbelt sign. You may now turn the Airplane Mode off your electronic devices that are within reach. There is a two-hour time difference, so local time is three forty-five p.m."

The phone the attorney gave me for this was very different from the one I had. He'd said it took excellent videos and that it was one of the stipulations in Tiff's will. I had to have him help me figure out how to use it, how to upload videos to the places they needed to go, and how to find everything I would need while I was traveling.

It wasn't as if I was in the stone ages or anything. I had a phone, just not that great of one. What did I need all the bells and whistles for?

It was just to call, text, and check out social media. Now, though, it was going to be the window to my adventures, the way that everyone who followed Tiff would see her legacy live on. As the plane pulled up to the gate, I took a deep breath, let it out, and prayed that I wouldn't end up dead in some back alley.

CHAPTER TWO

Noah...

"Hey, kid," Ms. Myre said as I walked into Ruby's Roadhouse.

"Hey," I replied.

"Your booth is occupied," she said, and I looked at her confused. "Someone came in and sat before I had a chance to tell her it was reserved."

"That's okay," I said.

"You want your usual?"

"I do," I said, then headed toward where I usually sat.

My mom and Ms. Myre had been best friends growing up, and their moms were the same way. Mom used to work at Ruby's when she was in school. Most of the kids in our area of the city worked here. It was one of those family places that everyone knew was good to their employees and a great place to earn extra cash when you needed it.

I'd never worked here, though, but that was because I didn't have any free time. When I was six, my parents put me in t-ball, and the rest was history. Every season, when my team inevitably won whatever tournament or championship we were playing, we came to Ruby's for our celebration. As I got older, the wins became a bigger deal. At twelve, it was the Little League World Series. In high school, it was state championships.

It sounds conceited when you expect to win, but it was what happened. From the very beginning, it was clear that I had some sort of natural talent on the field. My dad had played in high school and college, but he wasn't a star by any stretch of the imagination. Mom had some athletic ability, too, but she never pursued anything more than having fun. Something told them I'd be more, and they instilled in me a belief that I could win anything I set my mind on. Turned out, they were right.

When the draft came near the end of high school, we had to watch it here. There wouldn't be anywhere else that would make sense. It was chaos. There were so many cameras and so many people, it was surprising the fire department didn't kick everyone out. It wasn't like I was going to go number one in the draft or anything, but the scouts had been around. They watched practices and games, and the more they watched, the more that showed up.

Everyone was so proud of me and of what I'd accomplished, but it was just a game, and I had a great time playing. I didn't expect to go in the first round, but when the Seattle Cascades went on the clock, my agent got a call. He handed the phone to me, and I said, "Hello."

"Noah Hammel?" the voice on the other end asked.

"That's me," I replied.

"My name is Mark Watson," he said. "General Manager of the Seattle Cascades. I would like to officially notify you that you will be our pick with the next selection in the draft. Welcome to the Cascades baseball organization."

"Thank you, Mr. Watson," I said, not able to hide my smile.

"We look forward to negotiating a contract in the coming weeks," he said. "Until then, enjoy the excitement that is likely to happen in just a few minutes. You can pass the phone back to your agent now. We'll see you soon."

I'd handed the phone back to my agent and turned to look at my mom from where I sat at the table by the television.

"With the twenty-third pick in the first round of this year's draft," the announcer said. "The Seattle Cascades have selected hometown player, Noah Hammel. The Indigo City Anglers are now on the clock."

The whole restaurant went nuts. We were pretty sure I'd get drafted and even knew I might be picked up by my home team. What we weren't expecting was the high selection. Mom was crying, Dad was cheering, and I just couldn't quit smiling. It took four years before I actually played for the major league team, but the organization had been good to me.

Every Thursday I was in town, I came into Ruby's and had lunch. It was something that reminded me of simpler times. I wasn't a big deal here. Well, they didn't make a big deal of it, anyway. I was still the kid who grew up eating Ruby's ribs and made it big. Of all the things I could have done, playing baseball was the one that changed my whole life.

"Excuse me," I said as I got to the table.

"Oh, I'm fine," the woman said, working on her computer.

"I don't work here," I said, and she turned and looked at me. "This is usually where I sit on Thursdays. You didn't know, and Ms. Myre didn't get a chance to put the sign up, but would you mind if I joined you?"

"Um," she said, looking around at the nearly empty restaurant. "I mean…"

The pause made it clear that she was confused, but baseball players had superstitions, and this one was mine.

"I normally wouldn't ask," I continued. "It's just a superstition of mine. I won't bother you, and I'll even pay for your meal as a thank you."

She took a deep breath, then sighed and shrugged.

"Sure," she said, pulling her laptop closer to her and sliding her plate down the table.

"I appreciate it," I said. "My name's Noah."

"Heather," she said.

"Nice to meet you," I said, reaching my hand out.

She took it tentatively, and I shook it, then let go. It was hard to tell if she was just weirded out by my sitting here, if she was just busy with her work, if she was shy, or exactly what was going on with her, but I decided that I'd bugged her enough. So I sat and waited for my food to get here.

"Here you go," Ms. Myre said, setting my lemonade down. "Your food'll be up in a minute. Can I get you anything else, ma'am?"

"I'm fine," Heather said.

"Her meal's on me," I said, and she looked over the screen of her laptop at me. "I insist. I've interrupted you. It's the least I could do."

She looked at me a minute longer, then smiled.

"Thank you," she said, smiling.

"You busy?" I asked. "Or would you like to talk?"

"I have a vlog, with an accompanying blog, that I have to finish," she said.

"Then I'll leave you be," I said.

She looked at her computer, then looked back up at me, then back at her computer, and shut the top.

"I think I need a break," she said. "So, tell me, Noah. What do you do for a living that causes you to have a superstition to need to eat at the same table?"

CHAPTER THREE

Heather...

Tiffany had left me a letter with specific instructions to not open it in front of our parents, and to be very careful where I opened it. Her attorney told me he'd asked about the contents, but she'd told him it was a secret that we shared, something we'd always make sure the other one knew if anything happened to us. The writing on the envelope was definitely from a much earlier time, and the color was somewhat faded, but the wax seal on the back was still a bright red.

When we were sophomores in high school, we took this art history class. It covered a ton of different things, but the thing that drew us to the class was the fact that we'd get to try out some of the things they did years ago, including calligraphy, which had always fascinated us. Of all the things we learned, the coolest one was how to do a wax seal. You could use almost anything, but they were originally used with the ring of a noble to mark that it actually came from them.

We were most assuredly not noble in any way, shape, or form, but the thought of pretending we were queens was too tempting. One weekend, we found ourselves at the mall, and there was a stationery store we stumbled into. It wasn't something we'd planned, but we both found these little stamp-type things that were used for the wax seals. Of course, we bought them, as well as some of the fancy paper they had.

At home, we both took out our fountain pens and proceeded to write up our wills. It was a dumb thing, really, and wouldn't be useful in any kind of real way, but we wanted to make sure that everyone knew what we had wanted if we ever died. Of course, the envelope wasn't that. Instead, it was a letter she'd written to me after she'd been adventuring for a while. If I had to guess, I'd say it was from less than five years earlier at most.

Heather ~

I know you will read this in private, but if you accidentally opened it in front of anyone, shut it now and go to the bedroom or bathroom or anywhere else that's private before you continue.

Good, now listen closely. You are beautiful, smart, talented, and so damn kind, it's amazing. I never wanted to make things awkward between us, but I've loved you since we first met. I know you love me, too, but this is different. I love you the way a romantic partner loves someone. I know you don't swing that way, and I know you would feel terrible if you had to reject me, so I never said anything.

If you're reading this letter, though, I'm no longer around, and you don't have to turn me away. I wanted you to know, though and figured after my death would be the easiest way for both of us to get our wish. Me letting you know, and you never having to turn me down.

The thing is, I know that you are capable of so much love, so much compassion, and you care so deeply. I want you to find someone to love you the way you deserve to be loved. With the adventure I'm hoping to send you on, I would ask you to be open to that idea. Find someone who flips your switch, ruffles *your skirt, tickles your fancy. Doesn't matter who they are. I just want you to find your happily ever after, or at least your happily for now.*

We pretended to be princesses and queens, but you deserve to have someone treat you as if you are because I see you that way. On this adventure, I want you to have sex. Sex with a stranger, someone new, an old flame, doesn't matter. I want you to enjoy sharing your body with someone else, and them sharing theirs with you.

Don't die without that because it's well worth it. I can tell you're rolling your eyes at this, but I'm serious. Passionate sex is one of the best things in the world, and there is no reason for you to not have as much as you can as often as you can. Please do this for me.

I love you with all my heart,
Tiffany

I'd read the letter again just that morning and had pondered on whether I wanted to have any of that kind of "fun" that she'd called it. Obviously, that wasn't going to happen with Noah. He was a good ten to fifteen years younger than me. Still, I could pretend for a minute that I wasn't as old as I was and that he'd sat down because of me and not the booth I'd sat in.

"What's your vlog about?" he asked, not answering the question I asked him.

"It's my best friend's," I said. "She started it years ago when she started traveling. It's an adventure kind of thing. She passed away a couple of months ago and gave me access and a mission to continue her vlog for her."

"I'm sorry," he said. "About your friend."

"Thanks," I said. "It's still fresh, but I've been doing better lately."

"Adventure," he said. "Like what kind of things did she do?"

"The list is shorter of the things she didn't do," I said with a smile.

"She was almost fearless. You know that reality show where they stick a bunch of people on an island and pit them against each other?"

"Oh yeah," he said.

"She did that early on," I said. "I think that's what gave her the bug to travel. After that, she started using up as much vacation time as she could, going anywhere and everywhere, doing crazy things. It was an inspiration to a bunch of people, and that's why she started her website. She'd take video of what she was doing, then edit it and post it. She always posted after she left the location because she didn't once, and some dude found her. It was a pretty terrible thing, so she changed how she posted her updates."

"That's terrifying," he said.

"No joke," I replied. "It was the advice she gave me in her instructions. I'm working on the place I just left now."

"Where was that?"

"Chicago," I replied. "I'm sticking with the states for my first year. If things go well, and I see this as something I might want to do more of, I'll try somewhere else."

"Where all have you been so far?" he asked.

"This is just the second place," I said. "I'm from Illinois, so Chicago was the first stop. I've never been out of the state before, and still live in the same town I grew up in. I'd been to Chicago before, but she insisted that's where I needed to start. She's given me a list of places to go, and I've been just sort of picking them at random."

"Guess it was some kind of divine intervention that sent you here, then," he said, and his smile was dazzling.

"How about you?" I asked. "What do you do?"

"I play baseball," he said, and I sort of waited for the rest, but he didn't continue.

"I think I must be confused," I said.

"Oh," he said, as if he realized he hadn't explained it well. "I'm a professional baseball player. I play for the Seattle Cascades."

"Really?" I asked. "I've never met a professional athlete before. Well, I guess Tiff was a professional athlete of sorts."

"I mean, that show has a lot of athletic things you have to do on it," he said.

"It does," I said. "She had to do a bunch of training for it. Fortunately, she'd been doing that kind of thing for a while before she went on the show. She didn't win, but she made it pretty far. Then she went on another show that had them travel around the world with quests and all these challenges. She had such a great time doing both of them. She was always pretty adventurous, even when we were kids, but those shows gave her the bug to travel."

"What's the website?" he asked.

"It'd probably be easier to show you," I said, opening my laptop.

I navigated through my stuff to get to the main page, then turned it around to show him. He looked at it, scrolled down, and read things as he went. He smiled, then smiled more, then actually laughed, and my guess was it was the video she'd made sure was on the front page of her swimming with sharks in South Africa. She'd used an underwater camera and captured herself freaking out when one of the beasts came and brushed by the cage she was in. When I'd seen it, I'd laughed my ass off, and that was my guess at what he was watching.

"She sure did have an eye for some dramatic places," he said.

"That's true," I said.

He closed the laptop and slid it back to me just as the waitress came by with his food.

"Here you go," she said, sliding a giant plate of food in front of him.

There was brisket and ribs, macaroni and cheese, cornbread, potato salad, and baked beans. There was no way this guy could eat all of that because it was just so much food.

"How are you going to eat all that?" I asked, absolutely baffled.

"Need it to get me through the night," he said. "I expend a lot of energy on the field, so I try to get in here on Thursdays when I'm home. My mom and the owner are best friends, so this is like coming home to eat."

"That's kinda cool," I said. "I never really left home, so this is something I never thought of before. Guess it's the way things go when you travel."

"It is," he said. "Now, I'm guessing you're not going to be swimming with sharks any time soon."

"Not on your life," I replied with a laugh at how quickly he changed subjects. "I don't like swimming in pools, so jumping into a cage in the ocean with sharks sounds like a nightmare."

He laughed, deep and long, and it was a nice sound. I hated that I was attracted to him because there was no way that anything would happen. Honestly, I should have insisted that he sit somewhere else or get up and move myself, but I didn't want to.

"You ever been to a baseball game?" he asked, and I had to stop and remember how to listen. "Because I'm playing tonight, and I'd love to invite you."

"If I *have* been, it's been a while," I finally said. "But you don't have to go out of your way."

"Consider it another thank you for crashing your lunch," he said.

I thought about it and realized that I didn't have anything planned and that going to the game might be fun. In fact, it was exactly the kind of thing that Tiff would have encouraged me to do. It was like I could hear her saying, "*Take the risk.*"

"Sure," I finally said. "I'll have to go and stick my stuff at the hotel, but I could probably make it work."

"Perfect," he said. "What's your legal name? I'll ask that there's a ticket for you at will call. Unless you need more than one."

When he said the last, it was like he was hoping I would say no, which confused me. There was no way he would, or even should, be interested in me.

"Just me," I finally said. "Traveling solo, kind of like the rest of my life."

"So, you didn't leave a heartbroken partner at home?" he asked.

"No," I said. "That ship has sailed, unfortunately."

"Never say never," he said, and the way he smiled kind of made my stomach bubble.

"We'll see," I replied, hoping I wasn't being too forward but not wanting to get my hopes up.

CHAPTER FOUR

Noah...

"Still gonna need your name," I said, getting back to the question I'd asked earlier.

"Oh, right," she said, and I could tell she was a bit flustered. "It's Heather Quinn, with two 'n's at the end."

"Got it," I said, then pulled up the app we used to reserve tickets for friends and family. "I found a seat that's kind of in the middle of the row. Is that okay for you?"

"Sure," she said. "I wouldn't know if it was a good seat or not."

"Well," I said. "It's behind home plate, so you'll be able to see me when I'm up to bat, but not when I'm on defense. I wouldn't want to put you where you could see me closer on the field because then you'd be out in center field in the bleachers, and I'm not gonna do that to you."

"You can," she said. "Like I said, I don't really know anything about the game."

"My parents aren't coming to this game," I said. "They usually try to come to a few each home stand, but they're out of town at my sister's place since she just had a baby."

19

"Honestly," she said. "It's probably better that I not meet your parents."

"Probably not," I said, and meant it. "How about you?"

"What about me?"

"What's your family situation?"

"Oh," she said. "My parents are still living in Harrisburg. No siblings except Tiff, who my parents adopted when her parents died."

"Wow," I said. "She didn't have any family?"

"Nope," she said. "Her parents died when we were twelve. If my parents hadn't adopted her, she'd have gone into the system, and I didn't want that. We knew some kids who were in foster care, and they got moved around all the time."

"I feel fortunate to have had a big family," I said. "Like, if something happened to my parents, we had aunts, uncles, grandparents, the whole thing. Even if they couldn't help, my sister and I could have stayed with Ms. Myre."

"That's why I wanted her to stay with us," she said. "We were sisters before we lived in the same house. It wouldn't have felt right if she'd had to go somewhere else."

"I get it," I said. "I've got a ticket available at will call for you. You can pick it up anytime. Do you have a way to get to the stadium?"

"I have rideshare apps loaded on my phone," she said. "They should be able to get me there."

"They should," he said. "But I'd feel better if you didn't take one home."

"Why?" she asked.

"I've heard some things," I said. "Besides, I'll be there and can take you home if you don't mind."

She looked at me like she was thinking about it seriously.

"How do I know you're not the one I should be scared of?" she asked.

"Fair point," I said. "I can call my mom so you can talk to her, or you can ask Ms. Myre."

"I guess it would be okay," she said, but she still sounded hesitant.

"I get that I'm basically a stranger," I said. "And I'm a guy, which makes me more dangerous than a woman. But I promise you that I'm really a nice guy. I won't push, but would definitely feel better."

"How about you let me decide after the game starts?" she asked.

"That'll work," I said. "Let me give you my phone number and you can send me a text to let me know for sure. I won't get it until after the game, but I can rush through all the post-game stuff if I know you're waiting."

"Okay," she said, and she sounded like she still wasn't sure.

I didn't want to push too hard because I liked talking to her. She was intelligent, fun, and had a wit that was as quick as my dad's. Sure, she was older than me, but really, age was only a number. My guess was about ten years, maybe a few more. I was just twenty-four, so it wasn't like I was a baby.

Besides, I'd been with enough women that I knew what I wanted. Some of the guys gave me shit for the people I found attractive, but I honestly didn't care. I liked what I liked and didn't bash their likes, so it was kinda fucked up that they did mine.

"Make sure if you end up using the rideshare app that you let them know that you're meeting someone at your destination," I said. "And that you're sharing your location. You don't have to, but if they think you are, they're less likely to mess with you."

"I do that anyway," she said. "Another tip Tiff gave me. Said she'd had way too many close calls in her travels to not do that. We actually shared locations as it was, so it's not like it was a lie or anything."

"Good," I said. "I would hate for something to happen to you because you came to the game to see me."

"I'm pretty fit," she said, and she was right. "Took self-defense classes with Tiff a few years ago. She said it was for her, but I knew she wanted to make sure I would be safe. Now, though, I'm glad she insisted. Made me feel like I could travel and not be scared, or at least not as scared."

"Good," I said. I rattled off my number, and she looked at me in confusion. "That's my number," I said. "So you can let me know if you're going to take me up on giving you a ride."

"Oh," she said. "Let me put it in my phone. I'll text you now so you

21

have mine. But know that I won't hesitate to block you if you get rude."

She said it with a smile, and I was sure she was messing with me. Still, I wanted to reassure her that I was a gentleman, so I said, "Wouldn't blame you, but I'm not like that. I don't send dick pics or anything like that. I'll only respond to you to let you know where to meet me after the game. In fact, I'll have your ticket at the family and press entrance instead of regular will call. You can go there, and they'll give you your ticket. Then you'll know where to meet me when the game is over. Otherwise, they'll send you out onto the street."

"I'll be sure to remember that," she said.

"I promise not to leave you stranded," I said.

"Hey, Noah," Ms. Myre said. "You gonna eat or gab?"

"Oh, crap," she said. "I've been keeping you from your food. I should pack up and go."

"You don't have to rush on my account," I said. "But I do need to get this eaten, or I'll be a mess on the field."

"I'll let you eat in peace," she said.

"Unlike what I let you do," I replied.

"It was nice to talk to you," she said, and it sounded almost like a brush-off.

"I look forward to talking again tonight after the game," I said, making sure she knew I wanted to see her again.

"Okay," she said as she stuffed her laptop into her bag.

She reached into her purse to pull out either cash or a card, but I put my hand over hers. Looking at me, she then looked down at my hand. I wasn't sure if it was a look of confusion, concern, or what, but she pushed her wallet back into her purse.

"I got this," I said. "Like I said, I interrupted you. I feel obliged."

"Then I'm going to insist that I make it up to you," she said.

"I'll hold you to that," I replied, letting go of her hand. "See you tonight," I added as she slung the laptop bag over her shoulder.

CHAPTER FIVE

Heather...

I took a rideshare back to the hotel and tossed my stuff on the bed. Pulling open my suitcase, I wondered what to wear to the game. I wasn't sure what the protocol was, so I didn't know if I should do something a little nicer or if jeans would be sufficient. There were a couple of simple dresses I had that were fine for eating at a nicer restaurant but weren't Met Gala type dresses. I thought about one of those but then realized that it was April and wasn't exactly warm outside.

Instead, I pulled out another pair of jeans and then went rummaging through the tops I had in the bag. I had a handful of tee shirts, but they all had some design or another on them. When I packed for this adventure, I hadn't intended to need anything more than just what I brought, but now I felt like I needed to get something better. Grabbing my phone, I called the attorney to get some clarification as to what I could and could not buy with Tiffany's money. I could get it with my own, but if I could use her account, that would save me a bit.

"McKinley Law," the receptionist said when she answered.

23

"Hi," I said. "I'm Heather Quinn. I was wondering if I could speak to Garrison."

"Let me see if he's at his desk," she said. "Is this regarding yourself? Or someone else?"

"Both," I said. "He handled my best friend's will, and I have a question about the funds I have available to use for my adventuring."

"Oh," the receptionist said. "I remember this one. Let me get him on the line."

She put the call on hold, and I heard the Muzak they had playing in their system. It only took a couple of minutes before the call was picked up by the attorney.

"Garrison McKinley," he said.

"Hi," I said.

"Heather," he said before I even said who I was. "You have a question about funds, right?"

"I do," I said, knowing the receptionist probably gave him that information. "I'm attending a baseball game and don't really have anything to wear. I wondered if I should use my own money to get a top to wear to the game or if that was something I could use the card from Tiffany's account for."

"First of all," he said, and I could hear the smile in his voice. "The money isn't Tiffany's, it's yours. And while I would suggest you not go and get a bunch of stuff you'll have to haul around with you, getting something to wear to an event that is an adventure is well within the scope of the will. I just want to make sure you've kept up with notifying the bank of where you are so they don't flag it as fraud and shut the card down."

"I have," I replied, breathing a sigh of relief. "I did it at the airport in Chicago before I took off. I'll do the same thing each time I go to a different state."

"Perfect," he said. "You sound a bit nervous, though. Have you had any issues?"

"I do?" I asked.

"Just a little," he said. "Not that noticeable, but something I picked up on."

"I just had lunch with a baseball player," I said, then realized what I'd said. "I mean..."

"That's wonderful," he said, and he sounded like he was really proud.

"It was a total accident," I added, feeling like I had to explain it all so it didn't sound so trashy. "I was sitting at his regular table, but I didn't know. He asked if he could sit with me, and we talked, and he invited me to the game. And now I don't know what to wear because I don't think it's a date, but I'm not sure it isn't, either, and I don't have anything to wear."

"Take a deep breath," he said. I could feel myself spiraling. I tried to breathe deep, but it took a few times before it felt like I actually got it. "There you go," he said once I'd taken enough breaths to slow my racing heart. "The answer to the question is yes, you can get something to wear. I know that this isn't technically something for a specific event, but I think it falls within the spirit of the rule, so I won't have any issues with it."

"Because I can use my own money," I said.

"Heather," he said, and I stopped and listened. "Use the card for the account. It's fine. Trust me, a handful of outfits will not break the bank."

"Okay," I said. "You wouldn't happen to know what someone should wear to a baseball game, would you?"

"Unfortunately, no," he said. "That's not something I have any knowledge about. I say, wear something that's comfortable. Maybe layer, since it's still pretty early in the year, and Seattle tends to be on the colder side during the spring."

"It is pretty cool," I said. "Not as cold as winter at home, but not exactly warm, either."

"Get a nice shirt, but also a sweater or sweatshirt," he said. "That will be fine for the game, I'm sure."

"That's not too casual?"

"Heather," he said, and I could tell he was getting frustrated. "Stop trying to make it perfect. Just find something you like that you want to wear and that you can still wear after the game. I promise he's not gonna be concerned about what you're wearing."

I took a breath, held it as I counted to ten, and then let it out.

"Okay," I said. "I think I can do that."

"Good," he said. "If you need anything else, let me know."

"Okay," I said. "And I'm sorry."

"I understand," he said. "Have fun tonight."

He hung up the phone before I could say anything else, and I was sure he was exasperated with me. I grabbed my purse and headed out the door, leaving the mess on the bed that was my suitcase. I was sure I'd be able to find some store in the area and buy something to wear.

"Tiff," I said as I stepped onto the elevator. "I'm gonna need you to guide me, 'cause I don't know what I'm doing right now."

CHAPTER SIX

Noah...

"Why the fuck are you so damn chipper?" Swift asked me when I walked into the clubhouse.

"Just a good day," I said with a smile.

"You and that fucking rookie," he said. "It's like you both got laid for the first time or something."

"Awe, what's the matter?" I asked. Knowing it'd piss him off, I added, "Didn't you get laid last night?"

"Shut the fuck up about that," he said and threw his bag into his locker before stomping off.

"Uh oh," Hennings said with a smirk. "Must be trouble in paradise."

"I guess," I said, shaking my head. "Adams seems fine, though."

"Adams is unflappable," Hennings replied. "I think he'd be completely calm if the stadium was on fire and he was doused in gas."

Just then, the man we'd been speaking about walked in from the weight room, gave us a chin lift, and went to his locker.

"Unflappable," Hennings said, making his way over to his own locker.

I unbuttoned my shirt and put it in the locker, along with my shoes

27

and jeans, then dressed in my warm-up gear before heading down to the cages. I needed to work on my swing, and the hitting coach had asked that I meet him there early. Walking in, I saw several other players getting their workout in as well, so I went to a cage and waited my turn.

"Noah," Coach said. "Glad you came in early. Let me get this machine set up for what I want you to work on. Then we'll bang it out before you go on the field for some live hitting."

"Sure thing," I said, pulling my batting gloves out of my pocket. I put them on, stuffed the helmet on my head, and took my bat into the cage.

"You're seeing the high ones fine," he said as he angled the machine. "You keep swinging at the ball that's in the dirt, though. They're gonna keep throwing them at you if you keep it up, so we're gonna get that out of your head right now."

He'd set up some sort of covering that had this hole in it in front where the ball came out, but I couldn't see the machine behind it. I had no idea how the ball was gonna release. I heard the machine start up, and the first ball came right at me. Leaning back, I nearly fell over, trying to stay out of the way of the ball.

"Yeah," he said, and I could hear some of the guys laughing. "Now, let's get to work."

We did exactly that, him changing the speed and trajectory of the pitches coming from the machine until I was seeing every single one as it came across the plate. Over and over, he moved the machine, angling it this way and that. I couldn't see him, but when the ball came out, I was able to read it.

"Good, good," he said when he shut the machine off. "Let's get you on the field and see what you've learned."

Even though I hadn't done much, I was still sweating and could feel the burn in my arms from holding the bat for so long. Snagging my mitt, I headed to the field. I could hear the coach talking to someone else, getting them working on their swing.

For an April day, it wasn't half bad. Everyone thought it rained all the time in Seattle, but the truth was, we just had a whole lot of over-cast skies and drizzle year-round. Summer was when we'd get to see the sun, but sometimes, in the spring, Mother Nature would dazzle us with a brilliant day, and today was no exception. Sure, by the time the game started, the night would come in, and the temp would drop, but for now, as early as it was, the sun was high in the sky, and there was nothing like it.

"Hey, Hammel," Hargrove called, and I looked over at him with a smile.

"What's up, rookie?" I asked as I went to him.

He was behind the cage, waiting his turn, so we stood next to each other and watched the pitches and hits from the guys in front of us.

"Sorry about Swift calling you out like that," he said, low enough that I was the only one who could hear him.

"Not a problem," I replied. "I just think he's in a pissy mood. He gets that way sometimes, so you gotta just learn to ignore him."

"I guess," he said.

Swift was right about something, though, and that was that the rookie had been smiling a shit ton in the last couple of weeks. Sure, he was on the roster for the first time, and he was looking like he might just make this a real thing. After we lost Cammy to the fucking Dragons, I wasn't sure what the plan was for third, but the kid was showing talent.

"You're up," Huffman said as he came out of the cage at home.

"Hit 'em far," I said as the kid went in.

"He's got some mojo going," Huffman said once the rookie was out of earshot.

"Something," I said. "Not sure whether it's first-year hype or pure talent, but he's doing well."

"Bit of both, I think," Huffman said. "And then there's the girl."

"Girl?" I asked.

"She's been sitting in the stands," he replied. "Every game, before it starts, he goes and talks to her. She blushes, he smiles, she giggles, it's fucking ridiculous."

"You saying you never do that with Skye?" I asked.

"Nope," he said, and the way he said it told me he wasn't gonna let me try to convince him otherwise.

"That's too bad," I said. "Sometimes getting those goofy looks is the best thing."

"That so," he said.

"It is," I replied. "It's even better when you can get it out of them without them even realizing it."

"Now you're sounding like Becky," he said.

"Yeah, well," I said, shrugging.

The kid took a swing at a ball, hit it right in the sweet spot, and watched as it sailed all the way to the batter's eye.

"Nice swing, kid," Huffman said.

He came out of the cage, a grin splitting his face so much it looked painful.

"Thanks," he said, leaning against the outside of the cage.

I stepped into the frame, settling myself in the left-hand batter's box, and waited for Rodriguez to throw.

"What you want?" he asked.

"In the dirt," I said. "But also something I can hit. Don't tell me which is which."

"You got it," he said, taking a ball and starting to throw.

The first one was in the dirt, but it broke way too soon, so I knew it wasn't gonna be up enough to hit. Next was inside, and I got around just enough to slap it down the first base line foul. Another in the dirt, this one breaking much later, but I still laid off it. Pitch after pitch, in and out, up and down, and finally, after I thought I could tell what was what, he tossed something that moved in a way it shouldn't, coming back up at the last minute to cross the plate.

"Strike three," Hennings shouted. "Gotta watch out for those. They'll fuck you up every time."

He walked into the cage, slapping me on the shoulder before stepping into the other box to take his swings. I grabbed my mitt and headed down the line toward the outfield, where several of the pitchers were standing around. I needed to work on fielding just as much as hitting, although my fielding is what had kept me with the team the last season.

Ichigo gave me the chin lift he did when he said hello. He knew English and could speak it pretty well, but he also liked to be seen and not heard. It was a weird thing, but it made sense with his on-field persona. The mysterious master from the Far East was not nearly as mysterious to his teammates. Most of the bullpen guys were shagging balls, along with the starters that were off for the night. I settled into my usual center-field position and waited for some hits to come my way.

"'Sup?" Kors asked.

"Just working," I replied.

"You got a bounce," he said as a ball flew out toward us. "Someone new in your life, or are you just happy to see me?"

I caught the ball and tossed it back toward second, where the bucket was for recovery.

"Just a good day," I replied.

I didn't know what Heather was to me. She might be a date, might be just a fling, or might turn into something completely different. The hesitancy she showed made me curious as to whether she was fucking with me, but her eyes didn't lie. They showed interest, even if it was a fleeting thing that crossed them. I was just hopeful she'd come to the game, and maybe we could do something after, too.

"Now I know you're thinking about someone," Kors said.

"Just someone I met today," I said, not wanting to give anything away.

"She coming tonight?" he asked.

"Maybe," I replied, because I didn't actually know. "Hopefully."

"Hope so, too," he said, slapping my back with his mitt.

CHAPTER SEVEN

Heather...

"Welcome in," the woman behind the register said. "If you need help finding anything, just let me know."

It was a tiny little shop that was right in downtown, and I had walked into and out of at least a dozen already. The hope that I'd find something here was not high, but I figured I wouldn't find anything if I didn't actually look, so look, I did.

This store at least looked like it had clothes that weren't either super earthy or trendy or like they were trying to market to a crowd that was definitely not me. They had clothes that would fit me, not someone who had a super high metabolism and worked out daily, and there were some cute things that might work for tonight.

"You got something in mind you're looking for?" the store clerk asked.

"I'm not really sure," I said. "I'm going to a baseball game tonight. I was invited by a player. I don't know if it's a date or if it's just him being nice, so I don't want to be too fancy, but I also don't want to look frumpy, if that makes sense."

God, I was talking a mile a minute, babbling on and on. I was sure

32

the woman thought I was an idiot or something, but she smiled at me, rested her hand on my arm, and then gave me a little squeeze.

"Let's find something that you can layer," she said. "Something that fits you but isn't restrictive. Something that shows off your assets without making you look like a tramp. Unless tramp is the look you're going for."

The fact that she added that just made me laugh and sort of broke the ice a bit.

"Yeah, no," I said. "Not wanting to be trashy or anything like that. I just want to look nice enough without looking like I tried too hard. Does that make sense?"

"Come on," she said, guiding me further into the store.

She showed me a few shirts, some of which were not something I would ever even try to wear. But then she found this nice blouse that wasn't terribly fancy, had a nice soft feel to the fabric, and was just flirty enough, as Tiff would say, to cause a stir.

"I don't know if I can pull this off," I said, hesitating.

"Tell you what," she said. "Let's get you one in green and one in burgundy. You try them both on, see which one you like better, then we'll work on another layer. I think they'll really look nice on you."

"Okay," I said, still unsure of myself.

I took the tops into the changing room she'd opened for me, locking the door behind me and pulling my purse over my head to set on the bench in there. Holding the tops in front of me, I looked at myself in the mirror, trying to figure out which one I wanted to try first.

"Green," I heard and figured she knew what I was thinking.

Taking her lead, I hung them both on the little hook on the wall, pulled my sweatshirt over my head, then my tee shirt followed. When I glanced at myself in the mirror, I shuddered. I would most definitely not want to take my clothes off in front of Noah. He was so fit and I was so not. I wasn't exactly fat, per se, but I had more than my fair share of extra pounds that should have been shed long ago.

Shaking my head, I pulled the top off the hanger and pulled it over my head. The sheer layer that was over the more fitted part fluttered around as it settled on me. Pulling the hem down to my jeans, I looked into the mirror and was baffled.

"How's it look?" she asked, and I opened the door and stepped out. "Oh, that's cute. What do you think?"

"I actually like it," I said, turning and looking back at the mirror in the larger area. "It fits really nice, and I don't feel fat in it."

"You are not fat," she said, and I looked at her. "You're not. You might have a few extra pounds where you don't want them, but who doesn't? I know that we are held to such a high standard that we automatically assume we're fatter than we are. Even a woman with a great sense of herself will sometimes hear that nagging voice."

"Thank you," I said. "That's really nice of you to say."

"It's true," she replied. "I spent entirely too many days crying because I couldn't fit into whatever it was that was the most popular style. Now, as long as my ass is covered and my belly doesn't flop out, I don't care."

I laughed at that and realized that she had the right idea.

"You should try the other one on," she said. "Just to see which one you like better."

"Okay," I replied.

"While you're doing that, I'll grab a couple of sweaters for you to put over it."

We spent the better part of an hour figuring out the best outfit to wear to the game. It was sunny out, but it was early afternoon. I knew that once the sun set, the chill would come in. I didn't know how close to the water the stadium was, so I figured that could also make it cold and damp. We settled on both blouses, figuring I could wear the other one later, and added a sweater, some gloves, and a jacket with a hood.

Once we had everything rung up, though, I saw the price and wondered whether it would be better to put it on my own card rather than the card for Tiff's business. In the end, though, I went ahead and used that card, figuring I could send money to it from my bank if I needed to.

As the cashier was bagging up my stuff, she asked, "What is your undergarment status?"

I hadn't even thought about that, and she could tell when she saw my reaction.

"Here," she said, grabbing a card from the register area. "Go here and talk to Melody. She'll get you set up with something that's comfortable, but will still look good when you undress for that sexy ball player."

"I don't intend on doing that," I countered, but she insisted.

"You never know how the night's gonna turn out," she said. "Better to be prepared than wish you'd been."

I nodded, knowing she was right, but still sure that they would remain my secret. Stepping out of the store with my bag, I turned the card over and saw that the store was just a couple of steps down the street, so I walked over and stepped in.

"Welcome in," the woman behind the register said. "Are you Heather?"

"How did you—"

"I got a text," she said, holding up her phone. "I'm Melody, and you're in the right place."

She walked me toward the back of the shop, pulling things as she went, and I was amazed at how she just knew what, where, and why with everything that was hanging around. When we got to the changing rooms, she opened the door and handed me the lot.

"Keep your panties on when you try the bottoms," she said. "If you don't get them, they'll be fine. I took a guess on size, but if anything feels tight or pinches, let me know and we'll adjust. Same if something is way too loose. I'm a fairly good judge, though, and got your size in the text, so we should be good to go."

I blinked at her, completely baffled at how quickly she made a pile of stuff for me to try on. I shut the door, put my bag on the bench, and hung up the items. Looking at them there, though, I was sure it wasn't gonna work. I mean, they were slinky and sexy, and I was not either of those things. Still, it wouldn't hurt to have at least something to wear underneath. Might give me a boost of confidence.

Somehow, and I couldn't say whether it was the fact that she'd been sent my size or she was a magician of some sort, every single item fit. There were a couple that I looked at and put aside because there was no way I was going to wear anything like them, but the rest were at least decent in their coverage, and they felt comfortable when I had them on. I decided on just two sets to get, knowing that if I felt like I wanted to, I could come back and grab anything else that might work.

"I'll take these," I said, setting the others to the side of the register.

Melody took the two I picked, then looked through the rest and added another to the pile. When she saw me open my mouth to protest, she held up a finger.

"This one is on me," she said. "Normally, I don't go giving away stuff, but you need this boost. You've got a date tonight, and I want you to feel fabulous. Shower, put this baby on, spray some cologne or perfume on your belly button, and rock the world."

True to her word, she only charged me for the two sets I wanted and threw the other in without a charge, marking it on the receipt as a gift certificate. Smiling, she handed the bag to me, and I took it, sliding it inside the other one I already had.

"I'm gonna want to know how this worked out," she said. "That's the only price you gotta pay for that set. You come back and tell me how it worked out, and I'll consider it money well spent."

"Um, okay," I said, unsure why I was agreeing with this woman.

Her smile was such that I felt like we were friends, although distant ones, and I felt like I might actually be able to pull off the sexy outfit she'd gifted me. I got back to the hotel, dropped my bags on the bed, then undressed and climbed into the shower. As much as I wanted to think of myself as someone sexy, it just didn't happen. Making sure I was as clean as I could be, I shaved my legs and armpits, something I hadn't done since, well, since entirely too long. Whether it would matter in the long run, I didn't know, but at least I was putting in the effort.

CHAPTER EIGHT

Noah...

"Why are you checking the stands so much?" Hennings asked.

"None of your fucking business," I replied.

"Well," he returned. "Excuse the fuck out of me. But, word to the wise, don't go fucking fans. It can lead to disaster."

"Oh, like you didn't go fucking the enemy's sister?" I asked.

"She started it," he said, but he was laughing.

"Whatever," I said, turning to look at the family section again to see if I could find Heather.

She'd texted me to let me know that she had made it to the stadium, thanking me for the ticket and that she would be in her seat well before the game started. The grounds crew was just pulling the last of the cages off the field, Houston having finished their batting practice, and I was just sort of hanging out and waiting. I'd already changed into my game uniform, the black jersey with black pants, and I just wanted to see what she thought.

Finally, after what felt like years, I spotted her coming out from the Diamond Club entrance. She looked at the field, then turned and saw me. I could tell when she did because she smiled and blushed. I walked over toward the backstop to talk to her.

"Hey," I said. "Glad you made it. You look good."

"Thanks," she said, her blush darkening. "I just feel like I might be either over or under dressed, and I can't tell which."

"Nah," I said. "You're dressed perfect."

"I had some help at the store," she said. "I didn't really have anything that would work, so I went shopping. I feel like I did okay with what I picked."

"You've got layers," I said. "Always a good choice in the spring. Hope the game goes well and we win."

"Me, too," she said.

I could tell she was nervous, but there was absolutely nothing for her to be worried about. I was an adult, she was an adult, and I'd invited her to the game to watch me play. There was hope that we'd do something afterward, but it wasn't a guarantee. I didn't want to force her or feel like she had to do anything she didn't want to.

"Good luck," she said. "Or, is that bad luck for me to say that? I know it's bad for theater stuff, but I don't know the rules about sports."

"It's all good," I said. "You being here is all the luck I need."

"Hey, Hammel," I heard someone shout and turned to the dugout to see Decker beckoning me over.

"Gotta go," I said. "You staying after so we can get dinner?"

"I mean..." she said hesitantly.

"If you don't want to, it's fine," I said, but I couldn't entirely hide the disappointment. "But I'd love to treat you."

"I think it's my turn to treat you," she said, and it was like she found a little burst of confidence in that moment.

"Whichever," I said, not wanting to force the issue. "You can text me at the end of the game, and we'll make a plan."

"Okay," she said just as Decker shouted my name again.

"See you soon," I said, then turned and headed toward the dugout.

"New friend?" Decker asked as I got to the dugout.

"Maybe," I replied.

"You know the rules," he said.

"Didn't meet her here," I said. "I don't believe that she knows anything about the game, so it's not like she'd have ended up here without my invite, so I think I'm good."

"Just be careful," he said. "We don't need another incident like what happened with Becky a couple years ago."

"Yeah, no," I said. "I will not be putting myself into a position where anything will make headlines. I stay as far out of the news as possible."

"Good," he said as he slapped my shoulder, then headed out to the bullpen with the starter for the game.

The rest of the team was still in the clubhouse, so I walked down the tunnel to wait for the start. All I wanted to do, though, was go back out there and talk with Heather. I had a thing for older women and wasn't sure when it started. Could have been the fact that my sister was older than me, and she and her friends always hung around the house. They would come over and do whatever it was that teenage girls did, and I would be practicing or working on skills in the backyard.

When you're in middle school, and your sister is a freshman in high school, there's this big difference in who you are and where you are in life. All my sister's friends were hot. Maybe not exactly, but to twelve-year-old me, they were very hot. They'd do parties and sleepovers and stuff, and I was always there, seeing them, listening to them talk about boys, and knowing that I wasn't on their radar.

By the time I reached high school, I had filled out some, and the friends of my sister, who were then seniors, started to notice me. It pissed her off, but what was I supposed to do? She forbade me from hooking up with any of them, told me she'd tell our parents, and that I'd be banned from playing ball. There was nothing that would take baseball away from me, so I never crossed that line with her friends. I wasn't a virgin but wasn't exactly experienced, either.

After I was drafted, I was thrust into a much deeper pool of women who wanted my attention. Most of them were older than me since I'd just graduated high school, but some were a bit closer to my age. I was careful, never wanting to put my career in jeopardy, but it was hard to hold off. I'd talked to some of the older players about how to navigate that whole thing, and the best advice was to stay away from them or just do one-night-stands, making sure to wrap myself up with my own product, not lead them on and make sure they were on the same page before I did anything.

Now, though, I was much more selective, carefully selecting women who were not at all interested in a relationship. Heather was different, though. She didn't come to me, wasn't looking for anything, and seemed like she was a really nice woman. I wanted to get to know her and build a relationship with her, but that was going to be hard if both of us were traveling. There was hope, but it was tentative.

"Let's go," our manager said, then led the team to the dugout.

We headed up the tunnel, dropped our gear onto the bench, and started our work on getting ready for the game. There was stretching, working with the trainers on any issues we'd had, and getting our tosses in to stretch our throws. Huffman and I worked well together, and it was almost an unwritten rule that we would warm up together. He was on the warning track just above the dugout when I stepped up, and he tossed me the ball to get things going.

All the pregame festivities went on behind us, and we were ready to stand on the top step of the dugout, or just on the field in front of the rail, for the national anthem. After that, we dropped back into the dugout and waited for the kid they'd chosen to say those magical words—"Play ball," and we were out of the dugout again and heading to our positions.

As if it were destined to happen, the first pitch was hit by the Dragons' center fielder right at me, and I drifted back to catch the ball without any issues. Tossing it back in, I wanted to know if she saw me, if she knew it was me who had caught the ball. It was distracting, so I had to push it out of my head and focus on the game instead of what may or may not happen after.

The top of the first was quick, just a handful of pitches, and we were heading back to the dugout to get ready for the bottom of the inning. I wasn't hitting until the seventh, so I sat on the bench to watch the game, but ready to be up if we got that deep. When we got the first two batters on, with a single and double, I thought things might change, but after a strike out, a pop out, and a ground out, we were back on the field for the top of the second.

It was a fast-paced game, both pitchers hitting their marks, and the batters barely finding anything to connect with. By the top of the eighth, we were ahead by a run that we scratched out in the third, trying to keep them from scoring. We all had to be at our best, focused on the game, paying attention to the scouting reports on where to stand and what to watch for. We'd had to dip into the pen in the seventh after our starter felt some tightness.

Our old teammate, Mitch Cameron, was set to lead off the inning, and we all knew he was a threat to go deep. He'd done it many times when he played for us and had found his groove when he went to Houston. On the first pitch of the inning, Cammy connected, and it was coming well out and toward the wall. I tracked it, watching it in the roof of the stadium, tracking it all the way to the warning track. I timed my leap and snagged it just before it went over the wall. The entire world exploded once that ball hit my mitt.

We all learned to tune out the crowd, focus on the game, pay attention to our surroundings, and know that we couldn't let them influence us in any way. It's like we put on mufflers or something, drowning out the noise, feeling the way our body reacts, watching the important things. Once you're out of a play, though, you let everything back in, just for a second, as you celebrate what you did.

Tossing the ball back into the infield, I saw the pitcher give me a nod and slap his chest. It was all the thanks I needed because I was doing my job.

"Fuck," Huffman said as he passed me back to the left field position. "Didn't think you'd get it."

"Glad I did," I said. "It was gone, for sure."

That was all that was said and all that would likely be said, too. Sure, some reporter might ask about it, about whether I knew I was going to catch it or what I was thinking. It was the weirdest questions that always threw me. What was I thinking? *I'm fucked if I miss this catch.* But you can't say that on national television, especially when it's live.

If Heather asked me, though, that would be another thing. Maybe that would give us something to start our conversations on tonight. Just the thought had me nearly distracted when another ball headed my way. Fortunately, though, I still had my head somewhat in the game, and I grabbed the ball on an easy few steps to my left. The third out was a ground out to our third baseman, who tossed it to our first baseman, and we were heading back for the final ups before hopefully saving it with the Guardian. The next inning wouldn't go fast enough, but it would go, and I'd have to pay attention to keep it where it was.

CHAPTER NINE

Heather...

There were so many things going on in the game that I wasn't sure what to pay attention to. One minute, it was calm, everyone just standing around, and the next, the ball was flying out to the guys against the fence, far away from me. Noah had said he was going to be in the outfield, so I guessed that he was out near the fence. I tried my best to understand what was going on and kind of followed the crowd on when to cheer because it made no sense to me.

I did see when Noah was up and hitting. The picture they put up on the big screen was a great shot, and I wondered whether he always looked good or if I was biased. I'd taken some video of me walking to the stadium, some of the outside where they had a few statues up for past players, and some of the posh area where the richer people were.

The seat he got me was toward the middle of the row, so I had people on either side of me. I was also a few rows back, so there were people in front of me as well. I did shoot some video of the field when the players were warming up before the national anthem played, so I felt like I had a good amount of footage to work with. I even took some

43

of the game itself, but I wasn't sure what the rules were with the league on whether I could use those.

At one point, I headed out to use the restroom, making sure I went when the players were switching places. There were restrooms in the fancy area, so I did my thing, washing my hands before coming back out. I wondered whether I should get food or if the game would soon be over and it would spoil whatever appetite I'd have. I settled for just looking around the area.

When I headed back toward my seat, I saw there was a place set up where you could buy things that were team related. They had hats, tee shirts, and a myriad of souvenirs to choose from. I didn't want to get anything big, but thought that picking up something might help me to remember the event. They had a small stuffed creature that looked like a brown version of the abominable snowman, and I wondered exactly why they had that. Flipping the tag over, I realized it was the mascot for the team, and I just had to get it.

"You ready to go?" the cashier behind the stand asked.

"Yeah," I said. "I'm new to baseball, and it's my first visit to Seattle. I wondered if you could explain why this is the mascot for the team."

"Welcome to Seattle," she said. "He's Bigfoot. The name is the Cascades, which is the mountains to the east, and there are rumors that these guys roam throughout the area."

"Oh," I said, the concept making perfect sense to me.

"You want a bag?" she asked, and I shook my head. "Great. Total is twenty-one fifty-five."

I pulled out my card and slid it into the machine, waiting for it to beep to indicate it had finished the transaction. When it did, I pulled the card out and stuck it back in my purse.

"You want your receipt?" she asked.

"Will I need it if I don't have a bag?" I asked.

"Wouldn't hurt," she said, so I nodded. She handed me the small slip of paper that I stuffed into my purse as well. "Enjoy the rest of the game," she added as I walked away.

"Thanks," I replied over my shoulder, pleased with the small memento I'd picked up.

I headed back down out to the stands just as the crowd gave a loud cheer. Because I was standing in the walkway that headed to the stands, I was in the perfect spot to see that the guy in the middle of the outfield area caught the ball just as it was going toward the fence. Since the fans were cheering, I figured we were the team that caught the ball, but I wasn't positive until I saw that the guy who was running from the field with the helmet on was wearing an orange jersey. I knew our team was wearing black uniforms, so that answered that question.

By the time I got up to the row where my seat was, the players were changing again, so the people in the row weren't too upset about me walking in front of them to get to my seat. I apologized for disturbing them, but they were all polite. I sat down just as the team finished their warming up, and the batter came to the plate for our team. I watched as he turned to look at the stands and realized it was Noah. I smiled, and he smiled at me, giving a wink. I couldn't help but blush. God, I was way too old for this kind of thing, but it was most assuredly boosting my ego.

He stepped into the square that was pretty much gone by now, taking a few swings of the bat before the pitcher got himself settled and threw the ball. It was so fast I didn't even see it come through, but Noah swung and connected with the ball. The crack it made when they met was loud. I stood, along with the rest of the crowd, as the ball went flying. I lost it in the lights, so I looked down at the players on the field. The guy that was furthest to the right was looking up and watching, and that's when I saw the ball land over the fence and into the stands.

The crowd went crazy, cheering so loud it was deafening, and I joined right in with them. Noah took his time as he ran around the bases. I saw him as he went past the third one, slapping the hand of the guy from their team that was in the little box on the side, before coming back to home plate. He again looked toward me with a big grin on his face, and I was sure that mine matched his. I didn't even notice the rest of the crowd around me, sort of watching what was going on.

"I assume you know him," the woman who was sitting next to me said.

"We actually met earlier today," I replied.

"Ah," she said.

45

The tone she used made it sound like she didn't like that fact. I waited, wondering if she'd expand on her thoughts, but she just sort of looked back at the field. She was close to my age, maybe a little older, and I wondered why she was so strange with her words and tone. Tiffany would have called her out on it, but I was nowhere near as bold as my best friend, so I just let it drop.

I spent the rest of that inning second-guessing myself about everything I'd done, not just that day but the last few weeks. I'd taken a leave of absence from my job, left my house and my state, and flew halfway across the country. Now, I was sitting at a baseball game, watching a guy who was likely young enough to be my son play, and getting weird vibes from the woman next to me in the stands.

But the more I thought about it, the more I realized that I had nothing to be ashamed of, nothing to feel bad about, and nothing that would warrant ridicule from a complete stranger. So, I held my head up high as the final out happened in that part of the game and pulled out my phone to take a quick picture of the little mascot I'd purchased. I sent it to my mom, knowing she'd show my dad, and then said that I was having a good time. It was late back home. I figured she'd respond when she got up in the morning, but my phone vibrated almost immediately.

Glad you're having fun. We miss you but are so proud of you for taking this leap of faith.

It was just the boost I needed to make me feel better, and it also helped me to know that whatever I did, I had their blessing. It was something I'd worried about when this whole thing started, but the more I did, and the more time I spent away from home, the more I realized that I should have taken Tiffany up on her requests to come with her on her adventures. I'd missed out on so much, but now I was finally doing something that would likely change the rest of my life.

CHAPTER TEN

Noah...

The first pitch of the ninth inning looked like a giant beach ball as it came over the plate. I swung right through and belted it out of the park. It flew up and out and over the right field fence and into the stands. Much as we needed the insurance run, I was just happy that I got to show Heather that I did, in fact, know how to hit. Of course, their starter had been good, and getting the first run had been something of a fluke due to the error, but this one was all mine.

As I trotted around the bases, I kept my celebration small. I'd dropped the bat as I left the box, slapped the first base coach's hand as I rounded the base, kept my head down, and touched second before slapping the third base coach's hand on my way home. No one liked a showoff, and this team was notorious for taking exception to anything that even hinted at disrespect, so I didn't want to fuck up the next few at-bats for the guys behind me in the lineup.

When I touched home, I looked up at Heather, and she was standing and cheering with the rest of the crowd. I smiled at her, big as can be, and she was beaming back at me. I didn't know whether the family around her knew who she was or if they even noticed, but it didn't matter. She was happy, so I was happy.

47

"Nice," the rookie said as I went past him.

It was a nice hit, and I was glad I was able to add that run, but we still had to get through the heart of their lineup, and that wouldn't be easy. High-fives, pats on the helmet, and slaps on the back greeted me as I went into the dugout to drop my gear off. Hargrave got out on a pop-up to the catcher, then the next two struck out, so we were back out to pick up the save with Strawberry coming in from the bullpen.

He'd announced to the team this would be his last season, but he'd made sure that the news was not leaked to the press. We all wanted to have him make a victory circuit through the league, much like some of the other closers had done, but he didn't want that kind of attention. He said it was disrespectful to the rest of the team, but we didn't want him to go out without the honors he deserved.

I took a peek up into the stands and saw that Heather was watching the insanity that was the introduction to our closer and smiled. I'd have to make sure to tell her about the alternate name we used for him, just within the team. I ran out to the outfield, carrying the ball I'd use to warm up with Huffman, and we did our thing. The handful of tosses back and forth, the checking of the scouting report for those who were due to come up, and just generally getting ourselves back into focus.

Huffman tossed the ball back to the bullpen catcher who had been tossing with Adams, and we got into position as the ball was tossed around the infield. The first pitch was slapped foul down the third base line, so we all shifted a bit to our right, more toward left field. Just a step or two, but enough that we felt we'd be able to catch anything that was hit into the air. The next one was hit high but well foul the same direction. That was two strikes, so hopefully, Strawberry would strike him out. Sure enough, the batter took a big swing but whiffed, the ball making a resounding smack as it hit the back of Decker's glove.

"That's one," I said, holding up my index finger.

We all shifted toward right field since the next batter was a lefty. This time, the first pitch was slapped on the ground and came right between Hennings and Swift, although Swift did lay out trying to catch it. I picked it up and tossed it back in to Hennings, who was near second, keeping the runner at first.

All we needed was a double play and we'd be out of the inning. Our closer was a powerhouse, tending to have players strike out more than they bounced into any doubles, but he'd been known to throw a few. The thing was, he was a precision pitcher when he needed to be and knew so fucking much about the game itself that I wouldn't put it past him to throw one ball and have the game over.

We all positioned ourselves pretty much straight away, knowing that their third baseman, who was our former player at that position, was not inclined to pull the ball and tended to hit it right at the right spot. Of course, if the pitcher was gonna throw something that would make him pull his hands in or have to reach out, that could change things. That was the beauty of the game. Just because you tended to hit one way, it wasn't a guarantee that you would at any given at bat.

I got the notification that he was throwing a fastball just slightly outside from the pitch communication piece I wore, which was also worn by the catcher, pitcher, second baseman, and shortstop. It was what had been implemented earlier than originally intended due to this team's scandalous stealing of signs a few seasons earlier.

Everyone got set, Strawberry got set, and the windup and pitch went right where he wanted it, the batter swinging and connecting it on a slow roll down the third base line. It was slow enough that Hargrave wouldn't be able to get to it and throw anyone out, so he watched it roll. It just rolled foul before it hit the base. The rookie picked the ball up and tossed it back to the pitcher, and we all reset and went back to where we started.

Another fastball was called, same location as well, and I set myself to watch. This time, the batter connected a bit better, and the ball was further fair, headed right to the rookie, who took it and threw to Swift who threw to Matsui for the end of the game. The crowd went wild, and the three of us in the outfield came together to do our little thing. Then we headed into the infield to connect with the rest of the team and give congratulations all around.

All I could think about the entire time, though, was how quickly I could get out of there and meet up with Heather. I didn't know whether she was the kind of woman who would jump right in on anything physical, but I hoped to find out. I had the whole rest of the weekend, with an off day on Monday, to find out, though, and I intended to make the most of the time I had.

CHAPTER ELEVEN

Heather...

The end of the game was crazy, and everyone was on their feet the entire time. I was swept up in it all and stood along with them. Watching how the players moved around, finding the right place to be was fascinating. When the first player struck out, it was great, but then the next guy got a hit. One player even dove to try to catch the ball, but it skidded just past him and out into the outer grass area.

The players on the field had shifted, first to one side, then to the other. Now, though, they were back to the more central spot, although the one guy was at the base with the player from the other team. My guess was they did that to keep the guy from running ahead or something. Baseball wasn't exactly a sport I watched often, so the rules were almost always lost on me. It was something I was determined to change, though, because I wanted to know more about Noah, and this was a big part of his life.

When the next guy was set to go, the pitcher set himself up to throw the ball in. He did, and the guy swung, but the bat must have missed most of the ball because it trickled down the line of chalk on the left side of the field, rolling so slow that I was sure that no one

51

would get to it. The guy who was close to that base just watched it roll. It ended up going out of the field area, and that's when he picked it up and tossed it back to the pitcher.

Everyone reset themselves again, the runner that was on the first base going back, along with the guy who was up, picking up his bat to try again. It was fascinating watching them move around without having to be told where to go. Obviously, they'd probably been doing it for years, so it was second nature to them. Still, the fact that it was so clear they knew the rules, what was happening when, and how to react in each moment was incredible.

Once the batter was back in his box next to the home plate, the pitcher set himself up, looked out over his shoulder to the guy on first base, and then wound up and threw the ball. The batter took a swing, and it went almost to the same place, just well inside that line and right at the guy who was over that way. It was also hit harder than the last one and went right to him. He picked it up and threw it to the guy who was on second base, who then threw it over to the guy at first base.

The crowd erupted when the referee over there indicated that the runner was out. All the players came toward the pitcher, and the outfielders came together and did this little dance thing before coming into the inner part of the field to join the rest of the team. I knew that Noah was out in the outfield, so I watched them do their thing, not seeing what the rest of the team did. When they all got into the infield, they all started giving high-fives, fist bumps, and all manner of other greeting-type things as they made their way off the field and toward the place where they waited when they weren't on the field.

Watching Noah, he did all the greetings and ended up in front of the bench area, talking to a reporter in front of a camera. I waited, wondering how long I should hang out before he would be done, but then headed down the walkway toward the field. A few of the people in the front of the area were clamoring for an autograph, which he obliged. I worked to get down to the edge of the field, and finally, the crowd cleared up enough that I could talk to him.

"What did you think?" he asked as I stepped up to the edge of the stands, a net between us.

"That was really fun," I replied. "It's my first game, so I don't know that I followed everything, but it seemed like it was a good game."

"It was," he said, his smile broad. "I've gotta go do a couple of things before I can shower, but then I'll be able to head out. I don't know how long you can stay in the lounge area, but I'll check. I'll either text you or send someone to get you if they're closing it up. Does that work?"

"Sure," I said, my smile nearly as wide as his.

"Great," he said, sticking his hand through the netting along the edge of the field.

I took his hand, and he squeezed, his thumb rubbing in circles along the back of my hand. It was an intimate gesture, and I wasn't sure whether it was good or bad, but I did like it.

"See you soon," he said with another squeeze before letting me go.

I headed down the steps and into the area where I first came in, finding a place to sit and wait for a text from him.

CHAPTER TWELVE

Noah...

I'd done the post-game interview, knowing it was coming since my home run happened in the bottom of the eighth, and then walked over to talk to Heather. Her smile and just everything about her was what I wanted, and I couldn't wait to get done and out of there. I knew there wasn't a guarantee of anything more than dinner, but I'd have been lying if I said I wasn't hoping for something more.

Before I got into the shower, I asked one of the guys who works for the stadium how long someone could hang out in the lounge area. He'd told me that when they started to shut the stadium down, everyone had to get out of there as well. I asked if it would be possible for him to have Heather brought to the clubhouse or even the press room until I was done with my shower and getting things ready. He said he wasn't sure but would find out. I gave him her name and what she was wearing, and then sent her a text to let her know someone might come and bring her back so she wasn't surprised or confused, then jumped into the shower.

When I got out, there was a note at my locker that said Heather was in the press room in the back waiting for me. There was still press around, so I wasn't sure how I was going to be able to get in, get her, and get out. As I dressed, I tried to think up some way to get her, but nothing was coming to me. At all.

"Hey," I heard Huffman say behind me, and I turned around.

"Oh, hey," I said, seeing him standing there with Heather.

"He said it was okay for me to come in now," she said, a blush running up her cheeks.

"Yeah," I replied. "We're pretty much done and heading out. Thanks, man."

"No problem," Huffman said, a slight smile playing on his lips before he turned and walked away.

Heather watched him leave, then turned to me and whispered, "He's terrifying."

I laughed. I couldn't help it.

"He's intimidating," I said. "And that's a good thing on the field. He's really a nice guy, though."

"I wouldn't want to meet him in a dark alley, that's for sure," she said.

"Honestly," I replied, pulling on my jacket. "If I didn't know him, I'd be terrified of him, too. Especially now. He's bulked up some since the end of last season."

"Well, he's really scary looking," she said.

I slipped my arm behind her, putting my hand on the small of her back. She flinched a bit, more like a startle than anything, but then relaxed into it. Normally, I'm not so forward, but she'd mentioned that she had to travel for her vlog, so I didn't want to waste too much time leading up to anything that might happen. I was stepping outside my typical plan.

"What kind of food do you like?" I asked. "I mean, obviously, you like barbecue, but I didn't want to go back there tonight. They all know me there, so it would probably be awkward, anyway."

"I'm good with most things," she said. "I'm not a huge fan of seafood, though. We just don't have anything really good back home, so I never acquired a taste for it."

"How about Italian?" I asked. "There's a nice little restaurant close by we could go to. One of the players that was on the team before really liked it."

"That sounds nice," she said.

We'd made our way through the underbelly of the stadium, past the locker rooms, offices, and such, and were heading into the parking area for staff and players. Not everyone parked in the garage under the building, mostly just the players and staff of the team, as well as those associated with the local cable station that aired the games. A handful of players and staff were still milling around, but it was fairly empty when we walked in.

"I wondered where you guys parked," she said, looking around the space.

"When the old stadium was here, the players parked in the same lot as the fans," I said, remembering what my dad told me. "I guess they just put up some barriers to keep them separate, but they had this sort of gauntlet that they had to go through that fans could stand on either side of. I'm glad I never had to deal with that, though. Some fans can be wild."

"Oh, that sounds terrible," she replied, and I smiled.

"You're good with me driving, right?" I asked, having realized we hadn't discussed that.

"Sure," she said. "I have no idea where we're going and don't even know the city, so I'd get us lost before we even made it out of the parking lot."

Opening the door, I held it for her to slide into the front passenger seat, then closed it after she was in. I went around the front of the car and got into my seat, pulling my belt on once my door was closed. Pressing the button on the dash, the car started, and I put it in gear, heading for the exit. It only took a few minutes to get to Zoppa's, but the lot was almost empty.

"You sure they're open?" she asked.

"They're usually open this late," I replied, turning the car off. "Let me check."

I got out of the car and headed up to the door. It was open, so I stepped inside.

"We're just closing," the woman who was near the front said.

"Do you have anything we can get to go?" I asked.

"Let me check," she said, stepping from behind the counter and taking a couple of steps to the side toward the kitchen.

I heard her say something to whoever was there, heard a man's voice respond, but couldn't understand any of what they were saying. My guess was they were speaking Italian.

"Olissio says there's some lasagna he can box up," she said when she came back. "You just want for you?"

"Two servings, please," I said. "Thank you."

"You have cash?" she asked.

I pulled out my wallet and checked, seeing a couple of hundreds, along with a handful of twenties.

"I should have enough," I said. "Can I get a bottle of wine to take with me, too?"

"I'll need your ID," she said, and I pulled it out to show her. "You have glasses and an opener, or should I give you the Lambrusco that has a screw-off top?"

"No opener," I said. "At least, I don't think so."

She nodded, then used an old-school calculator to ring me up. I handed her both hundreds, telling her to keep the change. It didn't take long, and when she handed me the bag of food, it felt heavier than I thought it should. I peeked inside and saw there were a couple of bowls of soup, breadsticks, and a dessert of some sort, along with napkins and utensils. She put the bottle of wine in another bag and gave it to me as well.

"You sure this is all for me?" I asked.

"All for you," she said. "We can't keep it, so better to give it to someone who will enjoy it."

"Thank you," I said, reaching to grab another twenty.

"No," she said, her hand on my arm. "Nothing else is owed."

"Well, thank you," I said and turned to head out the door.

CHAPTER THIRTEEN

Heather...

Noah went to see if the restaurant was open, but he was in there a while. Finally, he came out with a bag that looked like it had more than just a couple of meals in it and another that looked suspiciously like it held a bottle of wine. He opened the back door, set the packages on the floor behind his seat, then shut it, opened his door and climbed into the front.

"They had lasagna," he said. "But they were closing. You want to come to my place? Or we can go to your hotel. Whichever you prefer. I could even just drop you off."

"My hotel is fine," I said, mentally trying to remember if I cleaned up after getting ready.

I was pretty sure I had, but would ask him to wait until I double-checked. The drive was quick, with us being in the city and it being so late. He pulled into a parking spot marked for guests and shut the car off. I took a breath, held it, then let it slowly out. This was it. The moment when I'd either make a fool of myself or find something wonderful. At least for a little while.

"Ready?" he asked and I nodded.

He got out, and I opened my door to do the same. I heard his door shut, the other one open and shut, then the sound of the horn as he locked it up. Holding the bags in one hand, he put his other one behind me, in the little dip right above my ass. Having not had a lot of dating experience, and my dates being from literal decades ago, I wasn't sure if this was just the new thing or if it was him actually wanting something more than just dinner. Either way, I was going to be open to whatever came my way as long as I didn't feel like I was being pushed.

We got in the elevator and headed up to my floor. The whole time, he kept his hand on me. I'd noticed when they put his information up on the big screen at the stadium that he was only twenty-four, which gave me some serious pause, but he might not know I'm that much older than him. I guess we'd have to wait and see when we got there.

When the doors opened on my floor, I tensed up. He must have felt it because he pressed his hand into my back, both urging me forward and moving me closer to him.

"Relax," he whispered, his mouth right next to my ear. "We won't do anything you don't want to do. I won't push you. Promise."

His breath on my neck sent shivers down my back, raising goose flesh down my arms and making my core heat, all things I had not experienced before. It was a new experience but was definitely one I was beginning to enjoy.

"I want to make sure I didn't leave a mess," I said, my voice husky.

"No problem," he replied. "I'll wait in the hall. Take your time."

I keyed my way into the room, and he stood still, keeping his word to stay in the hall. I flipped the little security latch thing so the door wouldn't close all the way, then turned on the lights. Thankfully, I hadn't left much of anything out, and when I checked the bathroom, it was clean as well, just the towels I used for my shower hanging over the rod. Going back to the door, I pulled it open, letting him into my temporary space.

"That was quick," he said, his smile bright.

"I must have cleaned up after myself," I replied as the door closed behind him.

There was a small table near the window, and he walked to it, setting the bag with the food down before carefully placing the bottle on it and then turning to me. I'd pulled my sweater off and set it on top of my suitcase, and when I looked at him, he had this fire in his eyes, a smoldering that I hadn't seen before.

"What?" I asked.

"Just enjoying the view," he said, and I could feel the flush run all the way up my body.

There were just a few paces between us, and he closed the gap, standing so close I could feel the heat radiating off his body, which sent shivers down my own. He raised his hand, brushing some of my hair behind my ear, his smile small but his eyes intense.

"Can I kiss you?" he asked, his voice so low I almost missed it.

Swallowing, I nodded, not wanting to break whatever spell he was under because this wasn't something that happened to me. This wasn't something that happened outside of romance novels or movies. No woman in her forties was hooking up with a guy in his twenties.

As he slowly lowered his head, I sucked in a breath, not quite sure why my body was reacting so intensely to him. We'd known each other for less than twelve hours, and he was already wanting to kiss me. No, this was a dream, and any second, I would wake up drenched in sweat from the fantasies my mind was playing.

He paused, just a hair's breadth away from our lips connecting, his eyes still intense, and waited, watching me. I had no idea what he was doing or what he was waiting on, but whatever it was, he saw it. His lips touched mine, and sparks exploded behind my eyelids.

My hands went up to his chest, gripping the shirt in my fists as his arms went around my waist, pulling me against him. What started off as soft and gentle soon grew into an intense thing that coursed through my body, igniting things I'd never felt before, and all I wanted to do was keep it going. I needed more of him, more contact, more touching, more... something I couldn't describe.

He hummed, a rumble that rushed down my throat as I opened my mouth to him. His tongue slid inside, searching my mouth, tasting every inch of it, and my knees grew weak. How I was still standing was a miracle, but he had a good grip around me. Sliding one hand down my ass, he pulled me closer, lifting my leg up along his thigh, then pressed himself against my most sensitive and secret spot. I could feel that he was not just playing at this. His apparent desire was pressed hard and long against me, and my God, did I want more of him.

CHAPTER FOURTEEN

Noah...

Her responses to my touches were more than I could ask for, and she melded against my body perfectly. Pressing myself tight to her, her leg on my hip, I felt her desire, and it just encouraged me further. Sliding my other hand down, I lifted her up, and she gasped, pulling back from the kiss.

"I've got you," I said, taking a couple of steps to the bed and setting her down. "I want to start with dessert."

Leaning over her, I watched her eyes, making sure I didn't move too fast or push too hard until I was sure she was comfortable. She was flushed, her eyes flitting back and forth between mine, wide with a mixture of surprise, confusion, and passion. I wanted to devour her entirely, but I would give her time to stop me. I wasn't an animal and could stop at any point, but I wanted her, and I wanted her bad.

"Noah," she whispered, and my name on her lips made my cock twitch.

"I'm not going anywhere," I said, brushing some of her hair away from her brow.

"I just..." she stopped, licking her lips.

"What is it, baby?" I asked.

She pulled her hands up to her face, swiped one down, closed her eyes, then took a deep breath.

"It's been a while," she finally said, her voice muffled by her hand over her mouth.

"That's okay," I said, realizing she was either embarrassed or nervous, but I didn't know which. "It's pretty easy to remember how things work."

"You don't understand," she said, and I wasn't sure if it was fear or what, but she was just lying there with her hands over her face.

I shifted to sit next to her, pulling her up to sitting, and tucked her against my body in a way that she wouldn't have to look at me but so I could hear her without her hands in front of her mouth.

"Talk to me," I encouraged. "I'm not gonna judge you, but I can't help if I don't know what's going on."

"It's stupid," she said, her voice low.

"Can't be that stupid," I replied.

With a deep breath, she let the air out, then said, "It's been about twenty years."

It took me a minute to realize what she was saying, but it still didn't quite make sense. When I didn't respond or say anything, she continued.

"I was in college the last time I had sex," she said. "I graduated a little over twenty years ago. I haven't been with anyone since. If you wanna leave, I understand."

Everything she said was in a rush, tumbling out of her like she had to say it quick or she would lose her nerve. I tried to do the math in my head, but it wasn't computing. What she was saying was that she was about twenty or more years older than me, but that didn't seem possible.

"How old are you?" I asked, and even to my ears, it sounded accusatory.

"Forty-four," she said. "You can leave if you want."

"I don't want to go anywhere," I said. "I just didn't realize there was this much of an age gap. You look amazing, and I'd have put you closer to thirty."

"Pfft," she puffed out. "There is no way you thought I was that young."

I leaned a bit away from her, turning her to look her in the face.

"I don't lie," I said. "I knew you were older than me, but I never would have guessed you were even forty."

"Well," she began, her eyes looking down. "Now you know. Feel free to excuse yourself politely or just walk out. I know I'm too old for you."

"Hey," I said, tipping her face up with a finger under her chin. "You're not too old. I was just surprised, is all. I have no issue with the age difference."

"Sure," she said, drawing the word out. "Every guy in their twenties wants to be with someone who's old enough to be their mother."

She sounded incredulous like she knew I was lying. But the fact of the matter was, I wasn't. I appreciated older women. They knew what they wanted, weren't afraid to go after it, and honestly, were usually better lovers. Had I been with someone as old as her? No. But that didn't make me shy away, either. Instead of telling her all of this, though, I decided to show her.

Slowly, I leaned down, carefully pressing my lips to hers in a soft, sensual kiss. She was stiff at first, but the longer I moved my mouth on hers, the more she relaxed until she finally opened her mouth to my tongue, and I deepened the kiss, pouring as much passion as I could into it. The hand I had behind her steadied her as I twisted, lowering her to the mattress, never breaking the contact between our lips. When she was flat, I shifted my body, sliding a knee between her legs and settling there, pressing against her. She gasped, feeling how ready I was for her, and her eyes popped open.

"I told you," I said, pulling back from her. "I was just surprised. It doesn't change how I feel at all."

"I almost left the stadium," she said. "When I saw the thing on the big screen that said how old you were. I really thought about it."

"I'm glad you didn't," I replied, holding myself above her. "You okay? With this, I mean?" I motioned my hand between us as much as I could. "Do you want me to stop?"

"Only if you want to," she said, and the red returned to her face. "Not at all," I replied, leaning down to kiss her again.

CHAPTER FIFTEEN

Heather...

I didn't want to admit what he was doing to me, but it was something I'd never experienced before. It was like every time I'd ever been with anyone else, they were just filling a space. With Noah, though, it was like everything exploded. Nerve endings were more sensitive, places that I'd long thought were dormant came alive, and my body was on fire.

Before I left home, I went to my doctor to get a complete physical—blood work, a mammogram due to family history, and a complete exam. She told me I was perimenopausal, which didn't surprise me. I'd had irregular periods for the last few months, so I expected it. She'd given me a couple of pamphlets as well as a website to see what things I might experience and told me to reach out if I had any questions.

Reading some of the things in those materials made me laugh because I wasn't at all sexual or even remotely enticed toward anything in that direction. If I'd found the right guy, I might have been more interested, but no one ever came along that made me want to even explore that side of myself.

Now, though, I understood everything it was talking about. My desire for him didn't even start until I'd gone shopping if I was being honest. I mean, I wanted to look nice, but when I was sent to the store with the sexy underthings, all of a sudden, there was a possibility, and I didn't even know why I wanted that.

With his body pressed against me, I wanted nothing more than to experience a connection, one that I'd read about in books, watched in movies and TV shows, and never even thought would happen to me. I wanted him, though. Not just anyone, but him. The man who interrupted my lunch because I'd sat at his table, the one who bought the same lunch, and who invited me to a baseball game to watch him play.

Letting go of every inhibition I'd ever had, I gave myself over to the pleasure that was coursing through me. I let myself experience this in its fullest, and returned the passion he was pouring into me back to him as much as I could. My hands slid up and around his neck, my lips parted more, and I spread my legs to give him direct access to my core, a place I didn't even realize could experience the pain and agony of being empty.

The more I opened up to him, the more he pressed me into the mattress, and I realized that there were too many layers between us. My hands pushed on his jacket, and he lifted himself up, pulling it off and dropping it on the floor. While he was doing that, I sat up a bit, working the buttons on his shirt, exposing his taut chest to me. It was like I was looking at one of those trashy romance novels I loved to read, with so much muscle under perfectly flawless skin. All I wanted to do was stare at it, run my hands up and down it, and feel it pressed against my own flesh.

His hands were on my hips, sliding under the fabric of the shirt I was wearing, pushing it up my body. I raised my arms, allowing him to pull it over my head, and watched as it landed on the floor with his own. I didn't dare look at him, not that I didn't want to. I wanted to know what he thought of me, of my body that was far too old for him. What he pictured, and whether I measured up in any capacity.

I didn't need to see his face, though, because he leaned down and pressed his lips against my throat, gently laying me back on the bed. His lips left a trail of fire down my body, just light touches that sparked like lightning wherever they landed. My throat, my collarbone, my sternum, and finally, he pressed them against the bra I had on.

It was at this moment that I was thankful that the women suggested I get something nice for underneath. If I hadn't, it would be a very utilitarian garment he would have been looking at, and it likely would have turned him off more than anything else. I didn't have long to let the thoughts tumble in my head, though, because he was moving his mouth lower and lower, still, closer to the edges of my jeans.

Staring down my body, I saw him look up at me. I didn't know whether he was making sure I was fine with what he was doing or if there was something else he was looking for. His warm breath washed over my abdomen, and I realized he was waiting for me.

"What?" I asked, my voice low and husky.

"I'm just waiting for permission," he said. "I'm not going to push you. You're in charge of this, but I want to keep going. I can smell your arousal, and it's driving me mad."

The thought of him smelling me made me uncomfortable, like I stunk or something. He must have seen my emotions because he leaned forward again, his body covering mine, his arousal pressed against me again.

"You have no reason to be worried," he said, his mouth close to mine. "You smell delicious, and I want to taste you. Can I do that?"

CHAPTER SIXTEEN

Noah...

I could see the apprehension on her face, and I wanted to do everything I could to wipe it away.

"You smell delicious," I said. "And I want to taste you. Can I do that?"

I waited for her answer, my cock twitching against her with each beat of my heart. It took everything in me to hold still and wait, watching her for an answer. She nodded, just barely, but I wanted her to say the words.

"Tell me," I said.

She licked her lips, her tongue almost touching my own lips.

"Say the words," I encouraged. "Tell me you want me to taste you."

"I do," she said, the words a whisper.

I waited longer, willing her with my eyes to tell me what I wanted to hear, telling me she wanted me to taste her, to dive my tongue into her very essence, to dine on her response to my touch. It took a minute, maybe more, before she finally said the words.

"I want you to taste me," she said, still in that barely there volume.

"That's my good girl," I said, undoing the button on her jeans.

As I lowered the zipper, I continued to watch her, waiting to see what her response would be as I removed the barriers between us. Her eyes were wide, wonder and fear an equal mix in them, and I had to remind myself to slow down. If what she'd said was true, then she'd not been touched in entirely too long, and I didn't want to push her too fast.

She let me lift her hips and pull her jeans down, showing me the matching panties to her bra, which was a very pleasant surprise. They were black, lacy, and had some gold threading through them, which was not what I'd expected. Not that it mattered what she wore, but seeing these things and that she made an effort gave me a little boost.

Dipping down to my knees, I pulled her jeans all the way off, setting them aside with the rest of the clothes we'd already discarded. I hooked my arms under her knees and pulled her toward the edge of the bed, eliciting a little squeak from her as she shifted with me. My hands rubbed up her thighs toward her panties, but when I looked up at her face, I could tell she was not yet ready. It was a miracle she'd let me get this far, what with us having hardly known each other for more than a few hours.

"Hey," I said, raising up. "You okay?"

She bit her lip, worrying the flesh between her teeth. I could tell she wasn't, but also that she didn't want to disappoint me, either. Shifting, I pulled her down onto my lap, wrapping her in my arms.

"We don't have to do anything," I said, and I felt her tense even more. "I promise. I'm fine with eating dinner, maybe a little cuddling, and getting to know each other better. How does that sound?"

Her face was in the crook of my neck, and I felt a slight wetness slide down as she sucked in a breath.

"It's okay," I said. "You said it's been a while. This was probably a case of emotional and physical overload. I get it. Let's get some of that lasagna while it's still warm, okay?"

I reached over and pulled my shirt from the pile, wrapping it around her shoulders. She shoved her arms through the sleeves at my urging, pulling the edges of the front together around her.

"You look pretty good in my shirt," I said, hoping that would lighten the mood some. "You looked pretty good out of it, though, too."

"I'm sorry," she said, her voice low.

"Hey," I said, tipping her head up to look at me. "You're just fine. You don't owe me anything. If you're not ready, it's completely fine."

"But you're…"

"I'm fine," I said, even though I wasn't exactly. "I'll survive."

Her eyes looked into mine, back and forth between them. I held steady, her on my lap, my shirt around her, and waited for her to see that I meant what I said. She must have seen it because she sort of let out a ragged breath and nodded.

"Come on," I said, shifting her to standing. "Let's eat."

CHAPTER SEVENTEEN

Heather...

I felt horrible. I was sure he was uncomfortable, what with his dick hard as it was. But his eyes told me he really was fine with me stopping everything. It wasn't that I didn't want to do anything. It's just that it had literally been almost twenty years, maybe even over that, since I'd done anything at all. The most I'd ever done since college was try a vibrator that Tiff got for me. It had been awkward and uncomfortable, so I just stuck it in a drawer and promptly forgot all about it.

He'd pulled the food out of the one bag, setting everything out on the little table for us to choose from. There were two bowls of soup, two boxes with the lasagna, and another box that was some sort of cake. I grabbed a couple of the glasses that they had set up near the sink to pour the wine into. Not exactly classy, but it was what we had, so we went with it.

Eating had really helped to settle my nerves. The soup was delicious with its spices and vegetables all blending together to make something I'd never tasted before. It was thicker than most of the soups I had at home, but those mostly came from a can, which I added water to, so it was to be expected.

72

When we got to the lasagna, I was careful to not overindulge. I didn't want to make myself so full that I would be uncomfortable. Besides, all the rich foods I'd been eating lately had been doing a number on my intestines. The last thing I needed was to have to excuse myself to the bathroom, shut the door, and have a blowout. Not exactly romantic in anyone's book.

Besides, I wanted to try again with him. I was feeling much more comfortable after being with him for the good hour or so we'd spent eating and drinking. The wine also helped me relax. I was careful to not drink too much, just one glass and not even the entire thing. I wanted to be in the moment, not drunk and unresponsive. Last thing I needed was him taking advantage of me if I went overboard.

"What're you thinking?" he asked.

"Just how good this all is," I replied. "And how I haven't eaten this many rich foods in a long time. The wine is nice, too. It's making me more relaxed."

"Not too much, though, right?" he asked, and I could see that he was thinking the same as me, that neither of us wanted to be so over the top that we weren't within our faculties.

"Oh, no," I said, holding up the little glass that was still mostly full. "I've been going slow. I don't want to get to a point where I can't make decisions for myself."

"Good," he said, taking a sip of his own.

His glass was about the same level as mine, so we were keeping a pretty good pace. Of course, he was bigger than me. Taller by a head or so and outweighed me by at least some. I wasn't skinny by any stretch of the imagination, but I wasn't exactly super tiny, either. If I had to guess, I'd say he had about fifty pounds on me, maybe a little more. I don't remember what it said when they showed him on the big screen, so I couldn't say for sure, but it seemed about right.

"So," I began, wanting to get to know him better in the little time I had left in town. "Why baseball? I mean, was it something you just kind of fell into? Or was it something your parents pushed you into?"

"A little of both," he said. "My sister and I were put into sports of all kinds when we were pretty young. We played soccer, basketball, and baseball. Neither of our parents wanted us in super high-contact sports, so we stayed away from football. I sort of just came by it naturally, excelling at each thing they put me in, but baseball was the most fun. I just loved the big field and the time I could take between pitches and players to enjoy the outdoors."

"That's amazing," I replied. The way he talked about it was like he'd always loved doing it, which was a good thing.

"What about you?" he asked. "Did your parents encourage you to try things out?"

"Hah, no," I said, the laugh coming naturally. "My parents wanted me to be happy, which is a great thing. But they really didn't try to steer me in any one direction. They made sure I did my homework and gave me free rein to choose what I wanted to try, but they never pushed me toward anything specific. I liked numbers and math and naturally excelled at that, so I did a lot of things like that."

"That sounds awful," he said, and I laughed.

"Not a scholar, eh?"

"I mean," he said with a shrug. "I did okay, but not anything like the honor roll. I passed my classes, didn't flunk or anything like that, but I was far from the top of the class."

"That's okay," I said. "I probably couldn't throw a baseball, let alone catch one."

"I bet you could," he said. "We should try tomorrow."

"Are you sure?" I asked.

"Absolutely," he replied, his eyes lighting up. "We can go to a park so it isn't like it's so stressful. Or, we can go to the stadium so you don't have to worry about an audience."

"Because the stadium won't have other professional athletes there to make a mockery of me," I said, rolling my eyes.

"Trust me," he said, his hand finding mine. "They won't make fun of you. We all remember what it was like when we first started out. We've also worked with kids and people who aren't athletically inclined, so they will leave us alone."

I wasn't sure whether I trusted that, but I trusted him, so I shrugged and nodded.

"First, though," he said, squeezing my hand. "We should have some dessert."

There was a spark in his eye, and I wasn't quite sure I was ready for all that we had started. When he pulled the final box over, though, I smiled. I could do cake. It was the rest of dessert I wasn't so sure about.

CHAPTER EIGHTEEN

Noah...

Between the wine and the food, she was relaxing well, and I was hopeful for a little more of what we'd started when we got there. I wouldn't push, but I'd have been lying if I said I wasn't hopeful. When I mentioned dessert, her eyes got big, so I pulled the box over, opening it up to share between us both.

"Here," I said, pulling a forkful from the cake that was in the box.

I held it up, guiding it toward her mouth. She opened for me, allowing me to feed her the small bite I'd gathered. I wasn't one to do the little couple things like that, but I wanted her to trust me, and this was a good first step. I fed her a couple more bites before she held a hand up.

"You need to eat some of it, too," she said. "It isn't fair that I'm the only one eating it."

"It's not something I like," I said, and it was true. "Don't get me wrong, I love desserts. I'm just not a big fan of tiramisu. If they'd given us gelato, it would be a whole different story, though. I don't usually share that."

"Good to know," she said. "Don't get between you and gelato."

Her laugh was light, and I really liked that she was relaxing again.

It had been tense there for a minute, but with the wine and food and now a little teasing, she was beginning to relax. Hopefully, that meant we would be heading to something more intimate, but I wouldn't push it.

"Most folks have that one thing that they won't share," I said. "What is your favorite thing to eat?"

"Oh," she said, surprised by my question. "I don't really know. I've never thought about it. I've been by myself or just with my family, so it's not like I have to worry about those sorts of things."

"Okay," I said. "How about this? If you could choose one food that you would never give up, what would it be?"

"Chocolate," she said without hesitation. "Absolutely anything with chocolate in it is something I would eat."

"Let's narrow it down a bit, shall we?" I asked. When she nodded, I continued. "You have a myriad of chocolate-flavored items in front of you. Which one do you pick up first?"

This time she took a minute to think, her eyes moving up and to her right while she sucked her lower lip into her mouth, and damn if I didn't want to pull it out and kiss it.

"I've never thought about it," she said, turning her eyes to me.

There must have been some kind of look on my face because hers brightened up, red rushing up from her neck to blush her cheeks in the most alluring way. She stammered a little, not really able to form whatever words were supposed to come out next.

"I think you'd taste really good covered in chocolate," I said, my voice lowering, my cock springing to attention again.

She reached into the box that held the cake and scooped up some of the cream that was on the top of the cake with her finger, swiped it onto her lower lip, and stared at me.

"Oh, baby," I said, moving from my chair on the opposite side of the little table to her side in a heartbeat. "I'm gonna need to clean you up now."

I leaned in, my lips very close to hers, eyes watching to see if she was cool with everything, but she closed the distance for me, pressing her lips to mine, her arms going around my neck, the creamy substance on my back, but I didn't care. She tasted of espresso and cream and sugar and cocoa, and I wanted to dive right into her.

I sucked the dessert from her lip, then plunged my tongue into her mouth, tasting every inch and loving the way the wine, lasagna, and tiramisu all blended together with her own flavor. Pressing upward, I pulled her with me, my hands going under her ass, raising her legs around my waist. Pulling back from the kiss, I looked down at the table, but it was too full, so I turned and saw that there was a desk on the wall across from the bed. The television was on the top, but there was still plenty of room next to her. I set her down and she gasped.

"It's cold," she said, and I realized it was much cooler than anywhere else.

"Hang on," I said, setting her on her feet.

I went over to the table, slid things around, tossed the trash into the bag, and set the dessert on the desk next to her before picking her up again and carrying her back to the table. I set her down where my place had been, then sat in the chair in front of her.

"I'm ready for my dessert now," I said, sliding my hands up her thighs. "You good?"

"I am," she said, her voice much firmer than it had been earlier in the night.

She spread her knees apart, leaning back some on the table so her hands were behind her, her breasts thrusting toward me, and it took everything in me to go slow, not just plow ahead and thrust myself into her. No, I wanted to make this last. I wanted to make sure she enjoyed herself and that she would never forget her time in Seattle. She'd said she had to leave within the next week or so to stick to the schedule that was required by her friend, and I didn't want her going without getting the chance to enjoy her to the fullest.

She still had my shirt wrapped around her, but it was open at the front and parted in the perfect way to allow me to see her sexy underclothes, ones I'd hoped she'd picked out just for me. I wanted everything in front of me, and I didn't know how long I could hold out until I plunged head-first into her.

The lights were on, the window shades open, and the view of the water was magnificent, but I only had eyes for the woman in front of me. By the time my hands reached her upper thigh, she was breathing quicker, and I could tell she was actually into what I was doing. I rubbed my thumb over her panties, right at the apex of her sex, where the bundle of nerves was the most sensitive. Her breath shuddered, her pelvis spasming under my touch. It wasn't gonna take much to push her over the edge, and as much as I wanted to go with her, I felt like she needed to go first, and often, before I got to my own release.

"You like that?" I asked, and she nodded, a little too fast, her lip going in her mouth again. "You keep biting that lip, I'm gonna have to make you stop."

She let her lip out, but her breathing faltered. Good. She was ripe and ready, and all I had to do was press the right buttons in the right sequence, and she'd be putty in my hands. While one thumb pressed against her clit, the other slid underneath the fabric of her panties, sliding in the slick her body was making, searching for the entrance to her core. I had to angle myself just a bit, but then I found what I was looking for, and my thumb slid inside her, her body going stiff before spasming around it.

"Oh, God," she said, her eyes shut tight, her hands gripping the edge of the table. "Oh, God, oh, God, oh, God."

She clenched around me, her knees trying to shut together, but my body was between them, so she couldn't. Her whole body sort of shook, spasming in one giant orgasm, the likes of which she probably hadn't experienced in quite some time. I'd stopped my movements, letting her flow through the experience until she settled back to where she'd begun. Using the hand I had been pressing to her clit, I reached around her waist, holding her body up as her arms gave way in the afterglow.

"You're absolutely breathtaking," I said, my voice low.

I held her against me, my arms around her, while hers twined around my neck, her head on my shoulder, her breathing becoming more regular with each moment that passed. Finally, after a few minutes, she sighed and pulled back, her eyes hooded with the after-effects of her orgasm.

"That was amazing," she said.

"I'm glad," I replied, pressing my lips to hers. "I don't want you to ever forget your time in Seattle. I'm hoping you'll plan to come back again, too."

"I kinda don't want to leave," she said, a bit of sadness in her eyes.

"You don't have to," I replied. "I can take care of you."

"But I do," she said, sadness tinging her words. "I promised Tiff that I'd see this adventure through. It's one year, and I gave her that. I would feel like I was betraying her if I didn't see this through, you know?"

"I do," I said, kissing her again. "Maybe we can plan to meet up in the next place you go. Either when I have games there or if I've got time off."

"I think I'd like that," she said on a sigh. "I don't even know where I'm going next."

"Let's not worry about that now," I replied. "Right now, we should just worry about you and making you feel so good you won't ever forget me."

CHAPTER NINETEEN

Heather...

He'd rocked my world, quite literally, and he was now being so kind it was a little weird. It was true that I didn't really want to leave. I mean, I'd never in my life experienced what he'd just done to me, and that both thrilled and terrified me. I never wanted the feeling to end, but I knew our time was short. I had about a week left before I had to decide where to go, book tickets, and get myself onto the plane.

"Where should I go?" I asked, his arms around me, his lips pressed against my forehead. "When I have to leave, I mean," I add.

I could feel his cock pressing against me, twitching in time with his heartbeat.

"Shh," he murmured against my skin. "That's talk for tomorrow. Tonight, it's about you and me and finding ecstasy."

He slid his hands under my ass, lifting me off the table. Walking slowly, he set me on the bed, then stood and headed toward the door. I was completely confused, wondering why he was leaving, but then the light overhead turned off, and I realized he was changing the mood, making it a bit darker. The only light that was left on was the one next to the table and the one in the bathroom, which was shining out into

81

the room. Was I that ugly that he had to have the lights off to be with me?

"Hey," he said, his smile brighter than the lights had been. "Figured I'd save us some time for later. Hoping you'll let me stay."

I let out a breath, thankful he wasn't going anywhere.

"I'd like that," I said.

"Good," he replied, then pulled the tongue of his belt through the loop. I felt my eyes go wide, and he paused. "You okay?" he asked, and I nodded but didn't take my eyes off where his hands were. "Should I put on a show?"

I looked up, then, and realized he was teasing me.

"Sorry," I said.

"Don't be," he replied. "You can watch all you want."

He sort of shifted his hips side to side, like he was swaying to some music I couldn't hear. I giggled because I couldn't help myself. Slowly, he pulled the belt loose from the clasp, letting the sides hang while he undid the button and zipper, taking ever so long to get through the process. Instead of waiting for him, though, I sat up straighter and reached out, grabbing his hands and shoving them out of the way. He let his hands go, letting me take control, and I didn't even recognize myself with how much I wanted to get his clothes off. It was like something had been let loose in me, and I had become a wanton woman.

Shoving his pants over his hips, they slid down his legs. He had boxer briefs on, and they were snug against him, but the bulge in front was very clearly ready for attention, and damn if I didn't just want to let it out and take it into my mouth. Moving my hands toward it, he grabbed my wrists, stilling me.

"You're gonna have to slow down," he said, his voice strained. "I won't last long if you go straight in."

"We've got all night," I replied but didn't know where the words had come from.

The smile that crossed his lips was breathtaking, and I had to sit back a bit and just take it in. He was so damn fine, hotter than anyone I'd ever dated, even when I was in college. And I was old enough to be his mom, which kind of freaked me out.

"I want to take my time," he said, taking my hands in his and leaning against me as he laid me down on the bed. "I want you to come for me over and over again until you're putty under my hands. Only then will I let myself go."

I was flat on my back on the bed, his warmth surrounding me as he pressed me into the mattress, his body over mine. My arms were above my head, and he slid both of my wrists into one of his hands, holding me firm there. I'd seen enough in film and read enough in books that being restrained could be a turn-on. I wasn't sure, but I was willing to give it a go because everything so far had been well above and beyond anything I'd experienced, and I'd enjoyed every little thing he'd done.

Running the hand that wasn't holding mine down the length of my arm, his eyes never left mine. He slid it over the material of his shirt, and I wished I'd thought to take it off. I wanted his skin on mine, every inch of the parts that were touching me, with nothing between us. God, I was wild with passion, and it was a heady thing to see it reflected in his eyes, looking back at me.

When he got to the collar of his shirt, he pulled it away from my neck, sliding his fingers inside the material to trace along my collarbone. The featherlight touch was such a strange combination with the intensity of his gaze. Shifting his body to the side, his hand went lower along my torso, sliding along the shoulder strap of the bra, something else I wanted off desperately.

"What are you thinking?" he asked.

"That I have too many clothes on," I replied, shocked at the honesty that came from me.

"Let's change that, then," he said, sitting up and pulling me with him.

He was kneeling on the floor between my legs, and he carefully pushed his shirt off my shoulders. I pulled my arms from the sleeves, shifting to allow him to pull it from behind and under me, then he dropped it on the floor in the ever-growing pile.

"Is that all?" he asked, and I reached around behind me. "Let me," he said, stilling my hand with his own.

With hands that were rough from the game but strong and firm, he slid them around my body, along the band at the bottom of my bra. His gaze held mine, never wavering, as he slid his fingers under the band at the back, unclasping the hooks that were there. I felt the material loosen around me, and a little sigh left my lips. His quirked up at the corner, but it wasn't a full-on smile.

"Should I take it all the way off?" he asked.

I nodded, and he let his hands pull the straps from my shoulders, the fabric sliding off and falling on the pile on the floor. Throughout all of this, his eyes never left mine. They held my gaze, captivated me, and I was bespelled by him.

"How's that?" he asked, and I struggled to find my voice.

"I want you," I said, then slapped my hand over my mouth, shocked and embarrassed by what I'd just said.

"That's good," he said, his smile growing. "I want you, too. Question is, how shall we start?"

My hands went around his neck, pulling his body flush with mine. I scooted closer to the edge of the bed so our pelvises lined up, hooking a leg behind him. I had no idea what I was doing but knew that I wanted him against me as much as possible, and this was a good place to start.

CHAPTER TWENTY

Noah...

Whatever switch I'd flicked had been precisely what she needed to relax and let herself go. Before dinner, she'd been a bit standoff-ish, like she was hesitant to move forward with anything physical, but now she was completely unashamed and taking the lead. Whether it was a ruse or just the fact that she hadn't been in a relationship didn't matter because she was now a very willing participant in the connection we were making.

Her arms were around my neck, her foot was at the base of my spine, and her pussy was pressed hard against my cock. All those things were what I wanted, but I knew I needed to get her off at least a couple more times before I introduced myself to the mix, so I slid my hands up her arms, around my own neck, and pulled her free. She looked at me, confused and a little hurt, which was not the reaction I wanted.

"It's still your turn," I said, and the confusion didn't leave. "You've been in a desert for a while," I continued. "It's time that I reintroduce you to the rain."

With her hands in mine, I clasped both wrists in one, then eased her down onto the bed. I'd wanted to see her breasts, but I wanted her to be comfortable first. Once I got her flat on the bed, I leaned over her, pressing my lips to hers. I'd had to come up off the floor, but that was fine because I kept my knee pressed against her, feeling her arousal through the panties she was still wearing.

"If I do anything you don't like," I said when I pulled back from the kiss. "You tell me, and I'll stop. Don't rely on me being able to read your unsaid emotions and needs, okay?" She nodded, and I smiled down at her. "That's a good girl," I said, and a flush ran up to her cheeks. "Do you like it when I praise you?" I asked. She nodded, but I didn't move. "Use your words," I said, waiting for her to answer.

"Yes," she said, her blush deepening.

"Good," I replied. "Because I intend to tell you what a good girl you are with every orgasm I wring out of you."

She shuddered just a little, and I knew I'd found her hot button, which was absolutely fine with me. Knowing what she wanted made it easier to give it to her. My free hand slid up from behind her back, caressing the skin next to her breast. Her quick intake of breath told me I was on the right track, and as my palm came across her breast, brushing against the raised bud of her nipple, she gave a shiver.

"Is that good?" I asked, and she licked her lips.

"Yeah," she said.

"You want more pressure?" I asked, doing just that. "Or should I be softer, with a lighter touch?" I decreased how hard I was pushing on her, letting her feel both options to decide what she liked best.

"Softer," she said, arching her back against my palm.

I let my hand slide over her nipple, feeling it strain against me and watched her face as she let the feeling rush through her. My knee was simply pressed against her, but she was shifting her hips, so I let go of her hands and slid that hand down, gripping her thigh so she stilled some, but also pressed and shifted my leg to rub against her most sensitive place.

"Oh," she said, her eyes wide.

The way I was standing wasn't gonna last long, as I didn't really have a good angle for much of anything, so I stood up, pulling my hands away from her, and she froze, staring at me.

"Gotta shift," I said, then nodded my head toward the head of the bed. "Scoot up for me, baby. I wanna be able to get to everything and still be comfortable enough to not crap out."

She complied, using her hands to help move her body up the bed, sort of in a crab walk fashion. She was on top of the comforter, and I knew enough about hotel rooms to know that I did not want to fuck on top of that, so I yanked it down to the foot, pulling everything but the bottom sheet with it.

"Whoa," she sort of squeaked, her eyes big.

"You don't want to be getting your sensitive bits on that," I said. "Trust me."

It took her a moment to realize what I meant, but then she made a face and went, "Eww."

"Yeah," I said, crawling up the bed to her. "Remember to tell me if you want me to stop, okay?"

She nodded, but I waited. I was near her feet, her legs tight together, like she was protecting herself. What I wanted was for her to be comfortable, not stressed out or anxious, but her body was saying things were feeling that way, so I waited.

"I know," she finally said after swallowing.

"If you can't seem to talk," I said, my lips curling in a bit of a smirk, and she matched it. "Well, then, you can snap your fingers or tap me. That work?"

"Yeah," she said, and the smirk stayed on her lips, which I liked.

Placing a hand on her ankle, I slid her foot to the side, making some space for me to move into. Once it was far enough over, I did the same with the other one. Her hands were by her hips, fingers splayed open. My first goal was to get them to squeeze up and bunch the sheets within them like she was holding on for dear life.

I wasn't experienced in all the ways to satisfy a woman, but I hadn't exactly gotten complaints, either. Heather was different, though. Most of the women I'd been with had at least known what they liked. It seemed she hadn't been given a chance to try many things out. My goal was to change all of that, though, and it started now.

Pressing my lips to the inside of her knee, she sucked in a breath but didn't pull away or make any other reaction. Slowly, with precision, I moved up her thigh, laying little kisses along the way. By the time I reached the juncture of her thighs, she was breathing in short bursts, and I worried she might hyperventilate, so I turned my eyes to her face.

She looked at me as if I had hung the moon and stars, like I had done some miracle she'd never experienced, and I was sad for her. Not really pity, but more like I needed to keep going, keep showing her that she was beautiful and deserving of love.

CHAPTER TWENTY-ONE

eather...

Every time his skin touched mine, I felt the electric shock of it all the way to my core. His kisses along my legs, his hands as he smoothed up them, and the way he looked at me when he turned his eyes toward my face, all just made me come alive. I'd never had anything like this happen before in my life, even when I was young and stupid, but now I was kicking myself for going so long without experiencing this, even a little.

"Don't stop," I said, and the smile he gave me was off the charts.

"Oh, I'm just getting started, baby," he said, his voice pitched low.

He was so close to my pussy I felt his breath as he spoke. He'd already sent me through the roof with his touches, but now his mouth was right there, right next to my most sensitive spot, and by all that is holy, I wanted him to kiss me there, press his lips against me, slide his tongue along my crease, delve into my core. I shuddered just thinking about it, and he chuckled a bit, a dark roll of sound that just made me shiver more.

"I love how you react to me," he said, smiling up at me. "I really want to taste you, but these panties are in the way."

He tugged on the crotch of them, a finger so close to me, but not doing anything I wanted it to. Raising up a bit, he reached up to my hips, gripped the waistband of the offending fabric, and began the slow process of pulling them down. There was no need to take it as slow as he was, but the smirk on his face told me he was doing it on purpose.

"You're terrible," I said, but my voice was light.

Finally, he pulled them off, but I wasn't sure it was exactly fair. I mean, he still had his boxers on, and I was naked.

"Are you gonna take those off?" I asked.

"Not yet," he said. "I've got other plans for right now."

Before I could even think, he bent down and slid his tongue along me, right where I'd wanted it, and I clenched my fists, pulling the sheets up into the balls. My head lolled back, and my eyes closed as I felt the heat rise through me as his tongue touched me. It was all I could do to hold on as he lavished me with his tongue. When he added a finger to me, sliding it into my core, I about came undone, feeling that pleasure rise and rise until it was coursing through me, my whole body coursing with it as wave after wave washed over me until I was falling back into myself, settling on the cool sheets.

"That was amazing," I mumbled, still feeling the zing of pleasure.

"And you looked amazing," he said as he moved up to lay beside me, an arm across my stomach. "Watching you fall apart was mesmerizing, and I want to watch you do it again."

"I don't think it's fair that I'm the one having all the fun," I said.

"If you don't think this is fun for me, then you haven't been paying attention," he said.

I looked at him and realized that he had a smile on his face that wasn't fake in the least. In fact, if I had to describe his mood just from his face, I'd say he looked pretty damn satisfied. He looked like he was more than just a little pleased with himself, and I wondered why that was.

"I think you've been without for entirely too long," he said. "Don't get me wrong. I want mine, too. I just want you to get more."

"What if I want you to give me more with that?" I asked, dipping my head in the direction of his dick, which was still straining against the thin material of his boxers.

"Oh, you want this?" he asked, cupping himself.

"I do," I said, and felt like a superhero with the way I was asking for things. "I've been wanting it since the first time I felt it pressed against me."

I knew I was blushing, but I didn't care. At this point, I was naked, he was nearly naked, he'd licked my pussy, sent me over the edge a couple of times, and I wanted to watch him lose control the way he'd made me. To see him in the throes of ecstasy at my hand. If I could give him even a little bit of the pleasure he'd given me, it still wouldn't be enough.

"Let me go grab a condom," he said, sliding off the end of the bed.

He picked up his jacket and pulled a strip from the inside pocket, then let the coat fall to the ground.

"You planned ahead, I see," I said, my smile likely making me look like a lunatic.

"I didn't want to assume," he said as he came back to my side. "But I didn't want to be caught without, either."

"Were you a Boy Scout in your past life?" I asked.

"Never," he replied. "But I do live by their motto of always being prepared."

"I'm very glad," I said.

While it had been years since I'd been with anyone, one of the things I always insisted on was the use of a condom. It was well past the time when folks knew better than to let themselves hook up without protection, not just from pregnancy but all those nasty things that get shared when you bump uglies. Thankfully, none of my previous partners, all three of them, balked at it, so I was for sure clean.

Still, I'd only known Noah for a day, not even, and the fact that he was going down on me without question gave me a momentary thought that he had likely been with several women. I mean, he was fucking hot. Not to mention, he was a professional athlete. Both of those things likely got him plenty of attention.

"Heather," he said, and I turned to look at him. "You sort of went away there for a minute."

"Sorry," I replied. "Kinda got stuck in my head."

"You wanna stop?"

"Not at all," I replied, snagging the condoms from his hand. "I think we have some work to do if we're gonna use all of these."

"I didn't intend to use them all tonight," he said, but the smile that crossed his face told me he'd give it a go if I was willing. "I'll need some recovery time between each one, though. You know, just so you know."

"Then we best get started," I said, tearing one of the individual packets from the strip.

"Yes, ma'am," he replied, and I glared at him.

"I am not a ma'am," I said, my tone firm. "I am nowhere near old enough to be considered a ma'am."

"Was using it as a term of reverence," he said. "Trust me. You're perfect for me."

I waited, but he reached down, sliding a hand between my thighs, and started stroking me. It was exactly what I needed to get out of my own head and back into the moment we were sharing. He didn't stop stroking, though, he leaned over, pressing his lips to mine softly, and that was all I needed to let go again and simply live in the moment.

CHAPTER TWENTY-TWO

Noah...

I'd peeled off my boxers, and she went a bit wide-eyed. Whatever apprehension she'd been feeling must have evaporated because she stroked me before rolling the condom down. I had hoped to get her off at least one more time, but she wanted me, and who was I to deny her that?

"You sure?" I asked, wanting to be absolutely certain that this was what she wanted.

"I am," she said and reached a hand around to guide me over her.

"If you want to stop," I began, but she interrupted me.

"Hard to stop something that hasn't started," she said, and I saw her point.

Settling myself over her, I guided my cock toward her entrance, slicking it along her slit before finding my goal. I went slow, pushing in just a little bit. When she sucked a breath in, I stopped, watching her.

"Like I said," she said, looking at me. "It's been a while."

"You lead," I said, staying just barely inside her.

She hooked a foot around my ass and pressed with her heel. I moved in as she gave me pressure, but stopped when she did. It was a slow dance, but I was willing to wait and work at her pace. She was

93

just fucking stunning, her blonde hair fanning around her head. A little pressure and I pushed in, but stopped again. It was frustrating because I wanted to be buried deep inside her, but if I pushed too hard or too fast, it would likely not be any good for either of us.

"I feel so full," she said. "But it feels so good."

I couldn't help but smile and waited for her to give me the sign she wanted more. Finally, after an eternity, I was deeply seated in her, and her heat, even through the condom, was a welcome feeling. It was like I'd been waiting for this moment for longer than was necessary.

Her foot pushed on my ass, and I took that as a signal to begin moving. I was slow at first, easing out then back in, but she wrapped her other leg around me, pressing it into me as well, and I took it for the enthusiastic encouragement it was and picked up the pace. She arched her back some and flexed her hips, tilting her pelvis in time with my own thrusts. When her breathing became a bit ragged, I pushed harder, pounding into her with as much strength as I could, until I felt her pussy tighten up, her hands on my arms, gripping me tight. As much as I wanted to hold off, my own release followed hers, and I nearly collapsed onto her, catching myself on my elbows.

Our breathing slowed, and I pulled out of her, holding the condom in place until I was fully out before sliding it off. I leaned over to the side of the bed, but there wasn't a trash can there.

"Be right back," I said as I got up and padded to the bathroom, dropping the condom into the can in there. When I came out, she had rolled to her side and was watching me. "You good?" I asked.

"More than," she replied, her eyes hooded, her face flushed.

"Come on," I said as I got to the side of the bed. "It's important for you to go pee after. Gross and awkward, but necessary to ensure you don't get an infection."

Her eyes went a bit wide, but then she realized what I meant and got up and headed to the bathroom herself, shutting the door after she went in. I'd grabbed a washcloth when I was in there and used it to make sure I got all the bits off before I did as I'd instructed her to do. I heard the toilet flush, then the water start for her to wash, I assumed. She came out of the bathroom, looking a bit embarrassed.

"What's wrong?" I asked.

"Nothing," she said, but I knew it wasn't nothing.

"Hey," I said, reaching out to pull her onto my lap. "Talk to me."

"I just feel like, I don't know..." she hesitated, like she was trying to find the right words. "It's stupid."

"Nothing's stupid, baby," I said, a hand rubbing her back.

"This was one of the best nights I've ever had," she finally said. "But I feel sad that this is gonna be a short thing with us. I mean, I don't expect you to want to stay with me forever 'cause you're so young, and I'm so... not."

"Baby," I said, reaching my other hand up to turn her face to me. "I'm good with keeping this thing going if you are. I really like you, and you're really sexy."

"Oh my God," she said, rolling her eyes. "I am so far from sexy it's ridiculous. I'm a pudgy older woman, and you should be with some sexy young thing."

"Okay, first, you're not pudgy," I said, but she scoffed. "No, you're fit and healthy. There's nothing wrong with your body other than that I'm not inside it again."

She laughed, which was what I was hoping would happen.

"Second," I continued. "We can keep things going as long as you want."

"But I have to leave," she said, and I could hear the sadness in her voice.

"I travel all over for my job," I said. "In fact, I'll be heading to Texas on Sunday after the game. Got a three-game series in Houston before heading up to Arlington for a weekend series next weekend. You could go Dallas on Sunday or Monday, and we'd have a day and a half together between the series."

"Really?" she asked.

"Oh, yeah," I said. "I'd love that. I could show you some amazing things in that area. There's so much history there, so many sites to see. What do you say? Wanna go there with me?"

"I could do that," she said, her eyes sort of twinkling. "I mean, I have to leave here and have to go somewhere that's got at least one state between here and there, so that would work. You sure you want me to meet you there, though?"

"It would make going to Texas a little more bearable," I replied, my smile genuine.

She seemed to think about it, like she was figuring out the logistics of it all, mapping in her mind her next steps. When she looked at me again, she was smiling.

"What's that for?" I asked.

"I never wanted to leave my hometown," she said. "Tiff was the adventurer. Going everywhere, doing all sorts of crazy things. Now, here I am, sitting on a sexy guy's lap – naked, mind you – and I can't wait to go somewhere new and see it all with you."

"I find that a very nice compliment," I said.

"Is this rushed?" she asked. "I mean, we met today, and now we're making plans?"

"Maybe," I said. "But I'm comfortable with it if you are."

CHAPTER TWENTY-THREE

eather...

I had everything packed and was sitting in the lobby waiting for the courtesy shuttle to take me to the airport. Noah had spent every night with me and showed me so pretty cool places I wouldn't have seen if I'd never met him. He also made sure that I would never in my life forget my trip to Seattle.

Tiffany was my best friend, my soul sister, and she was taken away from me way too soon. But she didn't really leave me, at least not in spirit. I think she knew, deep down inside herself, that her life was going to be a bright flame racing to her end. She also knew that I'd never do anything wild or crazy unless she forced me to, and she wasn't that kind of person.

"Anyone going to the airport?" the courtesy driver asked in the lobby.

I stood up and wheeled my suitcase toward the door.

"I'll take that," he said, grabbing the big one I would check and the small rolling one I'd carry on, and slid them into the shelf after I'd climbed on the bus. "Which airline?" he asked, as I was the only one on board.

I told him, and he nodded, closing the doors and pulling out of the

97

parking lot. I watched as the hotel got smaller, thinking back over the last few days I'd spent with Noah. If Tiffany were here, she'd be telling me I'd done good. I'd faced a fear and met it head-on. My reward had been to find a man who I could enjoy my time with, realize that my body was something that could be worshipped and that heaven could exist here, even if I couldn't share any of these things with my best friend.

Wiping an errant tear from my cheek, I mentally thanked her for sending me on this adventure, as it started a whole new chapter in my life I didn't know was coming.

NOTE FROM AUTHOR

Images and Blurbs available upon request.
I would ask that you obtain high quality headshots and cover art images directly through me, rather than taking them from either my website or Amazon, however, blurbs are readily available through both places.

ABOUT THE AUTHOR

Born and raised in the Pacific Northwest, CM Kane was fed a steady diet of sports, particularly baseball. Having this love of the game instilled in her at an early age, she found that nothing was better than getting lost in the game. Storytelling was another gift that was encouraged in her youth, and she's taking to the written word to explore a new aspect to the game she loves.

Social Media and Website Links:

Website:
https://www.authorcmkane.com

Facebook:
https://www.facebook.com/AuthorCMKane

Instagram:
https://www.instagram.com/authorcmkane/

Amazon:
https://www.amazon.com/author/cmkane

BlueSky:
https://bsky.app/profile/authorcmkane.bsky.social

ALSO BY C.M. KANE

Seattle Cascades

1. Extra Innings

2. Caught Stealing

3. Backstop

4. Power Hitter

5. Double Play

6. Find a Gap

7. Sweet Spot (Coming Soon)

8. 7th Inning Stretch (Coming Soon)

New Orleans Magicians

1. Choke Up

2. Caught in a Pickle

3. Brand New Ballgame (Coming Soon)

4. Fan Interference (Coming Soon)

5. Flashing the Leather (Coming Soon)

Austin Aces Hockey Club (Shared World)

Power Play

Anthologies

Unnerving: Eclipse

Street Justice (Limited Time)

Fooling Around (Coming April 1, 2025)

Neon Lights & Country Nights (Coming June 1, 2025)

Stand Alone Titles

A Switch in Time